Copyright © 2018 by Victoria Beelik. All rights reserved

Published by Victoria Beelik
Santa Paula, CA

All rights reserved. No part of this publication may be reproduced, stored in any data system, or transmitted, in any form or by any means, electronic, mechanical, photocopying, recording, or otherwise, without written permission from the publisher. If you would like to use material from the book, prior written permission must be obtained by contacting author.

The author and publisher make no representation or warranties with respect to accuracy or inaccuracies. The advice and strategies written may not be suitable for all situations. Author will not be liable for damages arising from contents of this book.

Book design by Victoria Beelik and Carl Gage

All Illustrations designed and owned by Carl Gage

Book production by Victoria Beelik

Acknowledgement

Where would I be without my wonderful, patient instructors from the Western Pleasure, basic riding, and jumping lessons? I would be without this book to help me get through all the amazing goofy things that happened when I was learning about horses for the first 22 years. Thank you to all who laughed at me when I put my gear on upside down, backwards or too loose. Thank you for the lessons that taught me how to laugh at myself and the opportunity to laugh at my husband while he learned to stop, drop and roll when he started out riding.

My mom and dad always taught me that life is short and how important it is to live it. This is my way of living it.

Mom, Dad and Tom; you are awesome people and I love you for laughing with me when dumb things happen.

The "Do's" and "Oops"

of Horses

BUYING THE PERFECT HORSE

An hilarious shoppers guide for both the new
buyers and experienced horse folks

By Vicky Beelik

This book wouldn't be what it is without the amazing
Illustrations by Carl Gage

CONTENTS

INTRODUCTION

Whether we've been riding for years or just started, many of us have experienced more than a few of the scenarios written in this book. If you haven't experienced any of these comical situations yourself; well, that just means that you're still somewhat new to horses, but you don't have to worry because these will happen to you. If you are new to horses, you'll find this book very valuable. Consider this your preparation for what is about to come. Either way, I thought we had enough serious books out there that tell us what we need to do correctly and what we need to do to "fix" our problems. It's time to take horse experiences to a lighter side from finding your first horse to getting your first ride on a new horse.

My goal is to make you laugh out loud and laugh again when you can point your finger at someone and say, "I read about you!" or "Hey, is she talking about me?"

I do not mean to offend anyone by my consistent references to geldings versus mares. I ride a gelding, so my usual reference will be to refer to the horse as a "he". I guess I am a bit biased, since I've always been a gelding person. I do admit, I have a lot of "mare person" friends. If a mare doesn't go into season on my legs or try to kick my horse's left nostril, I am okay with mares. Heck, I ride an Arab so that explains a lot of my craziness.

I hope you enjoy this book as it was meant to be; lighthearted and somewhat sarcastic. I am not one to preach. I can honestly say that many of the subjects I touch on I have personally experienced.

I hope you enjoy.

CHAPTER I- FINDING YOUR PERFECT HORSE

The Search Begins with Self-Awareness

It all starts with searching for that perfect pony. So many choices: tall, short, dark, light, draft, Arabian, awake, asleep, two legs, four legs, and maybe even one that sings "Staying Alive". Then, there are the discipline choices that range from Western, trail, Dressage, Endurance, disco dancing, the Waltz, or maybe just an all-around horse that can do everything, including bring you a beer. Let's put the discipline aside for a moment and just focus on the general horse. What does your perfect horse look like and what would he do? How fast do you really want to go? How fast do you want to stop? Do you want a horse so tall you'll need a ladder to climb on? Do you want a horse so calm that your dog can ride him backwards? These are all very important questions that will need to be answered before you even start looking for that horse.

Let's start with the most important thing to look for in a horse, the color! The color is critical when looking for a horse, because that is what you'll fall in love with and that's what other people will see first. For many, color is the first and only qualification for their perfect horse. And why not? If you have a beautiful horse that everyone wants to pet, what else do you need? Who cares if it has no feet, bucks you off every time you try to get on, is missing a leg, or does nothing but stand and drool; it's beautiful!

Now that someone has finally brought you back to some level of reality, let's look at the actual factors to consider when shopping for your dream horse. For starters, you need to honestly evaluate your experience. After that, look at what makes up the perfect horse for you like the name, age, what the ad says (versus what it means) and geography.

Before the search starts, it's important to self-reflect about your personal experience and riding skills. Personally, I am perfect. I can ride anything from fast to slow, even the ones that dance on their hind legs... NOT. I used to train horses back in the day when I bounced instead of splatted. During that time, I realized a lot of people had very strong opinions of themselves. These people (usually people who've been riding for a really long time, like a year) are extremely experienced. They will be the first to offer to help you find your horse, train your horse and train you. Oh wait, I apologize, you may be one of these people. It's amazing how easy it is to turn a confident, experienced rider into a person who's face wiggles in the wind because they can't stop their potential "love of their life". So, are you extremely experienced and have the knowledge that can handle anything? Are you at trainer level? (This is defined as a person who has been riding for a year, has handled 1 horse and who has helped to lead a horse to a tie rail) Are you a laid back, semi-beginner who just wants to enjoy life? Or, are you a beginner who really shouldn't be on anything other than the horse that takes the quarter? No one needs to answer these questions out loud. Just quietly consult with the angel on your left shoulder and the devil on your right shoulder.

It funny that the more one thinks they are an experienced, "can handle anything" rider; the more fun it is to watch them ride a challenging horse. If you have a friend who has this high opinion of themselves and you are going with them to test ride horses, that's the time to take a flask full of something delicious with strong alcoholic content so you can really enjoy the show. Or, take your trainer this is when you will know if your trainer is truly a trainer or if they still need at least another month into their 1 year of riding to be an official "trainer."

Back to you, now. You've realized you may be a bit new for a reining, gymkhana (barrel racing, keyhole or pole bending) or bucking horse so you're going to start slowly with a "hang loose", let's be "BFF's" kind of horse. And of course, a gelding. (I warned you I was biased.)

What's in a Name

If you are new to horses and just getting involved in the horse world, you'll find the name of a horse to be very important. If you've decided to start mellow, you'll be looking for horses with names like: Sleeper, Wilbur, One Eye, Leaner, or Mellow Yellow. People say names don't matter. I believe in fully evaluating the name of the horse before moving forward. If the horse isn't named because of his personality, he may learn to live up to his name. Horses behavior doesn't always reflect in their name, but you'll be surprised at how often it does. The name of the horse can be a self-fulfilling prophecy.

We start with the name because this is the first part of the ad that you'll see as in the caption. When you see ads that have horse's names based on anything high energy, you may want to keep looking. You will see ads that say something like, "Caffeine Shot is an amazing, calm 11-year-old gelding." It doesn't happen all the time but, sometimes horses' names probably really do have true meanings. Some of these may be (but certainly are not limited to):

- Electric Rod (we'll call him "ER" for short).
- Sleeper: Does that mean you'll get to sleep while recovering from being dumped? Or does that mean all your friends will pass you on the trail and disappear over the horizon, while you negotiate with "Sleeper" just to get him moving.

- Sun: Well, his front legs may be reaching in that direction, but if you're a trainer that should be no problem.
- Moon: He's so fast, you moon your friends that are behind you because your pants fly off.
- Sky High: He was the offspring of Sun except he has Dressage training.
- Silver: Because you'll be hi whoa'ing a lot.
- Bolt: Translation self-explanatory.
- Lightning: You'd be better off with Electric Rod.
- Flash: You'll be passing your friends in a flash of light. There will be no brakes.

Another important tip is to not <u>ever</u> consider a horse named after a rap artist:

- Tone Loco- This horse is truly Loco. No telling which way you'll go, but it will be a surprise.
- Icey Tea- This horse will give you an Icey hop and jump each time you get on.
- Kan Ya West- No, but you'll be going East whether you want to or not.

I think you get the basic idea about names. Fast names can mean fast horses, rapper names mean you better be ready to get your groove on, and other names mean you have some options. The great thing about the name is that the next word is usually a word that says something about their beauty, like gorgeous, stunning, beautiful, sparkling………… you'll know better because you've gotten this far in this book.

Age Does Matter in the Horse World

The next consideration is the age of the horse. Believe it or not, age does matter (unlike ads you see on Craigslist). Do you want a young horse that can grow up with your children? Do you want one that's almost dead, so you can run as fast as he does when he takes off? Please stay away from equine jailbait. What defines equine jailbait is subjective to the experience of the rider. If you are a beginner looking for casual riding, jailbait is under the horse age of 23.378 years old. If you are a more experienced rider, jailbait may be 5. If you are a trainer, these days, jailbait seems to be 2 and the horse should be finished by 3.

The age of a horse can be deceiving. Don't be fooled by age. There are some 20-year-old horses that seem to thrive on Equine Viagra; they just go and go and go and go. Just when you think he stopped, he goes again, and you can't stop him if you wanted to. Sometimes, the ad says 20 years old, but later you find out they accidentally added the "0". That one is named "Lightning". There are some 5-year old's that are seasoned, mellow perfect horses. There are some 5-year old's that are perfect when given the horse version of a "dooby" and a good snack. Those horses will have high maintenance costs because you must keep them mellow and happy by giving a constant supply of the "special" hay that keeps them in chill mode. Age is a tough one. I recommend you find a horse that can still stand, remembers where the food trough is, doesn't walk into walls because he's blind, doesn't jump the sun or moon (not the name of the horse) when he sees a lizard, leaf, dog, piece of hay, plastic, or you. Despite popular opinion, vet checks can help. This is unless you found the perfect 75-year-old because he's beautiful.

The Secret Meanings of Ads

Now that you've eliminated about 75% of the horses for sale, the next step is really looking at the descriptions. It always makes me chuckle because the most common description of a horse for sale is, husband safe, sound, can ride front, middle or back, loads, trailers, ties, good with clipping, can be ridden alone and the famous "Bombproof". There will always be the special ones that bow, won't stop on command or can hop on two back legs.

There are so many different words in a horse ad that mean so many different things. Again, I could write a book on just this topic, but we'll summarize. Ads have their own secret translations that only a few very experienced people know the real meaning of. We are going to just cover the basic descriptions you'll see in these ads.

"Husband Safe" should mean you can put your "non-horse" husband, whom you love so much, on the horses back and he'll be safe. That may be true, but what else can it mean or what doesn't it include? In reality, this can often mean that you haven't decided how much you love your husband, so this may be a good way to get rid of him. Or this can mean that your husband will be safe, but your kids may need seatbelts to stay on, and an umbrella to slow down. Sometimes a husband safe horse means you're safe from ever seeing him again because your new horse just ran off with him, all the way to the next county.

When an ad says, "Loads and Trailers", it can be redundant because the horse needs to load into the trailer to bring him home, unless you live next door. These two terms can stand alone as individual parts of the ad. He may be great at loading into a trailer. He may jump in so fast, you will go with him since you're in front of him. This is usually a correct description for loading, but they just don't say how he loads. Sellers are still telling the truth, even when they must tie a long lead line to the horse through the front of the trailer and use a tractor to pull him in. They are still telling the truth when they need to provide him some of that high-quality illegally grown hay that leaves him very mellow along with a good munchie snack to lead him in. If this is the case, he'll probably fall asleep before he backs out. The question to ask is, "How does he load and trailer?" Do you need to hire a helicopter and drop him in from above? (You will need a convertible trailer.) Do you need a complex pully system to drag him in? Or, do you need strong calming drugs? Some to give him before loading him, and some for you after you've finally got him in the trailer.

The term "trailers" has its own set of fun meanings. Once you've reached your destination, you may find him standing backwards. You won't be able to assess how this happened because he'll be jumping over you to get out before you're finished completely opening the doors. It is not uncommon to see outward dents appear on your trailer while you drive home with your new horse. Don't worry, he's self-testing how strong his feet are. If he magically winds up in the back seat of your truck, you may have a problem.

"Ties" is another common word in an ad for a horse. How general can this be? He knows how to tie a knot? He ties for last in a race? If you don't already know, we all really hope you can tie a horse to a rail, tree or trailer. A lot of ads say that the horse "ties". The question is if they stay tied or know how to break their lead lines. Ties to what? Some amazing horses do know how to tie. They can teach your kids how to tie the perfect shoe lace. Of course, this is the same horse that will pull back at a tie rail and take off running down the road with the tie rail closely following. In this circumstance, you'll usually gain a lot of items that you could sell at a garage sale (if you don't get sued for theft) since he'll be collecting these on the attached tie rail that follows close behind him. Hey, if this happens, you could sell him with an ad saying "ties", you just don't have to say that ties mean he's good at dragging things down the road with something he's tied to.

The greatest ad line I've ever seen is, "Green broke". At least this ad is somewhat honest. This is directly contrary to "Experienced", but you'll be amazed at how many times this term will be used with "great potential" or "kid safe". Green broke means barely broke. The term (unofficially) comes from you landing in a pile of soft warm green "something" after your barely trained horse has launched you through the sky. A green broke horse that is a beautiful mover with amazing potential that clips, ties and trailers, and he is, without a doubt, the perfect horse for anyone. Do I really need to say more? Oh, yes, I do. This horse is probably named after a young rap artist, because he hasn't had enough experience to figure out his true nature. If he's pretty and you want to buy based on that, your trainer that has had 6 months of horse experience themselves, will be very happy.

Ads often describe the experience the horse has or had. Experience (can go front or back), reining, barrels, sleeping, used as a handicapped horse, used for kid's lessons, likes to jig, trail horse, front runner during a sprint in a one-horse race on a single trail track, top finisher at the drag races, sleeps through earthquakes, Dressage, etc. Experience is always important based on what you want to do but a good horse should be able to adapt to however you want to ride.

Some basic things to think about when the description shows experience. When you see an ad that says, "Sun was used for Gymkhana (barrels, pole bending, keyhole)", that usually means speed. Reining cow horse, Performance horse, race horse usually also means speed but add fast turns. Speed can be a good thing for someone who likes to go fast, not stop, doesn't like to ride with your friends because he will HAVE to be in front (and about a mile ahead). Performance horses are amazing athletes. These horses not

11

only go fast, but they turn fast. It would be like being on a ride where you hold on to the center and spin and spin and spin some more. Hope you don't get motion sickness. Don't get me wrong, not all speed trained horses continue to be competitive athletes. There are some that are darn tooting mellow. Those are usually the husband safe 75-year-old horses. It's a simple equation; if you want calm and safe, any horse that has training that involves speed is the opposite of what you're looking for. Of course, that is, unless he's really pretty and his name is "Rainbow".

Kid's lesson horses are interesting. Many times, these horses are a bit older and mellow. If you see an ad for a 5-year-old, husband safe, kid's lesson horse, that horse will be expensive because you'll have to support the habit that keeps him mellow. If you see an ad for a kid's lesson horse, you should wonder "why" this person is selling the perfect kid's horse. Or, Is he perfect? It usually doesn't say how long the horse has been a "kid's lesson" horse. Ad is correct but it's just missing a few words. It does skip some important details that should have been included in the ad... "Kid's lesson horse for 3 days. We found the kid 3 days later 17 miles away after he finally got the horse stopped, but this is a great "kid's lesson horse". Or, we bought him last week because we were told that he was a "kid's lesson horse" but we only used him once with a child. It took us 3 hours to get him out of the tree. There are truly great kid's lesson horses, but those are not for sale or rarely for sale.

There are a few other descriptions that I find humorous. Here are some of my other favorites:

- Cowy: Low to the ground, quick turns. Do you like to spin without planning? Are you good at landing when things disappear from below you?

- Great endurance prospect: I hope you don't want to stop, because, neither does he. Hope you don't want to ride slow, because, neither does he.
- Beautiful movement: This is almost like "all around". This horse could be the most beautiful mover in the whole wide world, on the ground. Watch and fall in love. This horse may be the most beautiful mover while on his back. Unless he is so smooth, you can carry an egg, in a glass of champagne with the glass sitting on top of another egg, his movement doesn't matter. Again, this may also translate to "turns really fast", "stops really fast", "dances on poles", "likes to do the Texas 2 Step". It's important to ask what their definition of a beautiful mover is. By the way, the beautiful mover's name is "Kan ya West".

I really love the description "an all-around". Some of these horses really have universal excellent qualities that make them the kind of horse that can do anything. Sometimes these ads mean we really don't know what he can do well, we know what he can't do but we don't want to tell you that. The best ad you'll ever see is: "This gelding is a great all-around gelding. He's been used as a performance horse, a race horse, a trail horse, he can do anything (but stop). No really, he's a great "all around" horse". This description can mean an assortment of things. This horse has done everything but was good at nothing. This horse was trained in a speed discipline but since he doesn't win, he's now "all around". Even though he is only 9 (he's really 32) he's so calm you can do anything with him. He's a great "all around" horse because he'd rather stand and be round (as in fat), than do anything that needs energy.

Without breaking the secret code to horse ads, you'll find the perfectly enticing ad to read something like, "Sky High is a 4-year old husband safe gelding that has been used for racing, barrel racing, and is now a kid's lesson horse. He can go on the trail for hours. He loads, trailers, and ties. He'd be a great first horse. Experienced rider required." This translates to, "Sky High is a 4-year old that will keep your husband safe from being near you because he'll dump him about a mile away. He's kid safe, when they are on the other side of the fence. He only turns left and you really won't ever need a trailer because you'll always be chasing him." Get it?

How Far will you Go

To many prospective buyers, the distance you need to travel to get your horse doesn't seem important, but it is in two different aspects. The first being how far he is from you so you can actually see him and assess him before finding out that he's deathly afraid of 1" black rocks. The second determining how much money you'll spend in that "special" grass hay to keep him calm during the trip home. There is one more thing, you need to see what kind of living conditions he used to.

Let's look at the geographical difference. It's a simple assessment. If the horse is almost perfect, will it cost you more to get there than what you're paying for him? Will you have to hire "Trust me, I'm perfect" Horse Hauling company to get him home? In this case, he better be perfect because you probably bought a horse you've never seen or seen just once. If you do have to hire a hauler to bring him home, I think it will be safe to say that you still don't know how he loads and trailers. Is he so close you can ride him home? You'd never know this is the same horse you see running with a rail behind him because you're now on his back. At least he knows how to turn around if he doesn't like your home.

The second consideration is the conditions he lives in. Why is this important? Because you need to know what he expects from you when you bring him home. This could make life easy or very expensive. You've qualified him from every other aspect, now you're looking at his living situation. If you are looking for an "all around, husband friendly trail horse", what do you think your new horse will think when you take him from a stall that has a heater, 3 feet of shavings, an electric blanket, and full access to only high-quality champagne, hay and organic supplements, and bring him home to a big dry pasture or a stall that has a cross breeze? I think he'll give you the equine finger and use his "beautiful movement" to get him back to the life of luxury he's used to. Does the horse live in a group with other horses? If the other horses are hiding in a corner far away, with bruises and wounds, while your horse is in the other corner smiling, eating all the food and smoking a cigarette, you may want to think twice about putting him with other horses. Of course, the only reason he may have been isolated was to keep the other horses from picking up smoking. Who cares they are fast enough to get away from him (because he already has COPD)? Or, since he's an all-around horse, he happily lives in a nice open stall, eating standard hay, one mare on one side, a gelding on another, and being fed carrots by anyone who walks by. This is a good horse to look at. Key things to watch for: Are the panels bent? If they are bent to the side of the gelding, he's macho macho man and still wants to be a macho man. If they are bent to the side of the mare, he's trying to figure out his sexuality. Don't worry, no matter what your gender is, he probably won't make a move on you. You're only two legged.

Making the Call

After thorough research, over assessment of the ad and comparison to the other ads you see for the perfect horse; you've found him and he is the perfect horse, his name is VaVoom, and you are going to call the seller. It's time to make the call. You know he's perfect because the ad said so. No, really, it said so. The ad read, "This is your beautiful perfect pocket pony who just wants to be loved. He's a great "all around" horse and husband safe. He will go anywhere you take him in just a halter. He'll do anything to make you happy". So, you make the call. The seller is so nice and so sad. She really loves him and doesn't want to sell him, but she has too many horses and her husband told her that she must downsize. She's had him for years. Your heart is melting, listening to the sad story and you prepare to explain what a wonderful life you will give VaVoom. It's important that you must qualify yourself, so they really know you'll give him a good home.

Once she takes a breath and stops crying, it's your turn to start asking the basic questions. You don't really need to ask the questions because you've already written the check (for about $500 more, just in case someone else wants him). You tell her that you're new to the horse world and not a great rider (unless you're a trainer, then you have already decided not to even waste your time). Here's about how the conversation and the brain pattern will go:

You: "He sounds wonderful, I can't wait to come out."
Seller: "Oh, he already loves you and he hasn't even met you."
You: "When was the last time you rode him and where did you go?"
Seller: "I rode him about 9 months ago, he did great. He walked around the trail like he'd just been ridden the day before."

You: "Oh? Why was it so long since you had ridden him? Was he hurt?" (Your heart melts, something is wrong with your new horse!)
Seller: "Oh no, that wasn't it at all. I've just been busy with my 75 other horses, so I haven't had time for Vavoom. He's so wonderful, you'll love him."
You: "What kind of bit do you ride him in? Did you ride him in his halter like the ad says?"
Seller: "No, not that time. I used a bit just in case because it had been so long since I rode him. I ride with a nice soft, high port, long shank bit. Sometimes he doesn't stop so I wanted to make sure I didn't wind up on the ground again. But, that was just because he spooked at a lizard. You know how scary those things can be."

You're sold!!!!! That's it; the seller has convinced you that he's a great horse. He's just what the ad said, the perfect husband safe pocket pony and he's close enough to go look at without having to ride him home or call "Trust me, I'm Perfect" horse haulers. It probably didn't matter what the seller said. The ad said he was perfect, and sellers are always honest. You love VaVoom and you will give him a perfect home and send the seller pictures of him regularly. You still need to meet him.

Taking a Ride to Meet Your New Love

Now that you are ready to look at VaVoom (and the other horses once you realize VaVoom is a green broke stallion), there are even more considerations to make before you really and truly fall in love. Since you've seen and ran from VaVoom, you've found another perfect horse at the seller's ranch. Surprisingly, he's also for sale because she has too many other horses. His name is Wilbur. Before writing the balance of the overpayment to the seller, there are some very serious red flags to look for from the time you arrive.

If you show up early to find the horse being fed a very strong margarita from a water trough, the seller giving him a dose of some type of liquid coming out of a brown bottle, the owner chasing the horse around the arena (the other horses will be laughing while drinking their martinis') or the horse is chasing the seller around the arena (the other horses will still be laughing and drinking their martinis) or you show up and see the seller dragging him out of the stall by his tail, you may still seriously consider him to be the right horse if you never plan to take him out of his stall. Best yet, if you see the whites of his eyes while he clings to the tree branch (the seller will tell you it was because of a big tiger that had just walked by), he may just be doing pull-ups. She won't tell you that your new horse won't tie to the rail. Horse is dancing around while the seller tries to saddle him. Of course, he'll be doing this dance to his favorite rap artist. It will be easy to cinch up once he steps over you and you're underneath. These are all strong signs to turn around, walk away and go get your own martini OR let your trainer/soon to be ex-friend get on him first.

Always ask the seller to get on your new horse first. When the current owner won't get on him before you, there will be a variety of excuses:

- They are injured (don't worry it's not from your beautiful new Wilbur).
- They want to see you ride him or her, so they can see if you are a good match.
- They just love to watch his "beautiful movement" and don't need to ride him.
- They are too heavy (that's why they are selling him. 94 lbs. is just too much weight) or, he already has a metal rod in his

back because they really are too heavy. On a good note, that will make it easy to climb into the saddle.

- He's too tall to climb on. (14 hands is tall, I must admit).
- They just rode another horse. This means they just rode him and got dumped. In this case, the owner met you in a golf cart because they can barely walk.
- They want you to ride first so you can see what he feels like "fresh". Fresh is the operative word. This is as in flying through the air like a water balloon only to crash on the ground, fresh off his back as soon as you climb on, or (best of all), fresh as in the fresh feeling you have after the wind clears you of all congestion because you weren't able to close your mouth when he was speeding down the arena with no brakes. At least you had a good bicep workout.

You've moved past the seller's multiple reasons they don't want to be on first. You've ignored the broken nose, arm and ankle. He's still the perfect horse. It's time to try him out for yourself. It's time to move on to the next round of purchase consideration steps. It's time for you to climb on.

Since you already know Wilbur is perfect, you have no problem taking him for a trial ride. The seller has generously offered to saddle him up for you. He is clearly excited you want to ride him. He stands perfectly still while they put the pad on him. You're impressed. The excitement clearly shows in Wilbur's eyes when he sees the saddle. Ya! He wants you to ride him. As the seller throws the saddle up to his back, Wilbur calmly steps to the side causing the saddle to come crashing down on the ground next to him. Two things could happen here: Wilbur watches with equine laughter because he totally did that on purpose, or he waits for it to land and uses that as an excuse to take off running, with the tie rail of course. In the second scenario, you would be amazed because the pad stays on as he disappears across the horizon. Let's just agree that Wilbur gets the saddle on with no problem. Saddle is on and cinch is tight. Don't worry about the kicking while the seller tries to tighten the cinch. It's probably because the flies really like to land in that area at the exact moment the cinch is tightened. The seller nicely explains how to "bob and weave" to avoid the hoof while the cinch is tightened.

The next step is the bridle. How tall are you? A well-trained horse, which Wilbur is, will only lift his head 1 inch higher than you can reach to get the bit in and bridle over his ears. A horse with a little more intelligence will raise his head exactly 2.17 inches higher than you can reach. It will be just enough for you to stand on your toes, stretch with your fingers, start cussing, and start negotiating with him to get him to manually drop his head for you. If he dropped his head for you, put it in his mouth himself and helped you put the rest of the bridle on, he wouldn't be for sale.

He's all set up and ready for the ride. Now it's time to get on. Here are a few scenarios:

- The calm ground mount: Even though you can't reach the stirrup with your left foot and you slide underneath him when you do finally get your foot in, he stands. Even as you use every muscle in your body to continue to pull yourself up, he stands until you're comfortably in the saddle.
- The "not so calm" ground mount: This is the same attempt as above, but he is way too savvy to just stand there and let you embarrass him in front of his mates, so he leaves the minute you slip underneath him. You're still there, looking up at the sky wondering what happened.
- Using something to get up with: This is simple, he's either going to stand there because you've just made it easier for him as well. OR, the minute you lift your foot to the saddle, he generously moves to the side, just far enough so you can't reach him. You'll wind up in the same place as you

20

would have if he'd moved off while you were trying to mount from the ground.

You're on and you're ready to go. I highly recommend you start in the arena. You'll make it safely to the arena because the seller holds the reins until you're in the arena, and the gate is safely closed so he can't escape. This is the time when you find out how well the brakes work. The ad said "soft" to the touch. How soft is soft? Well, he's either so soft he flies high and lands in a tree the minute you touch his side, or he's so soft that he really enjoys feeling the pressure of your heel on his side and pushes into it as hard as you push, ultimately landing you in the side rail. In this case, you may not have a new horse, but you'll have a nice bruise and *that* will be free. Sometimes "soft" means don't even touch his sides because he will take off at an immediate run. Forget the trot and lope, he's soft. A feather will trigger his fastest gate. Even though you're practically doing the splits to keep your heels out of his sides, the seller keeps yelling at you to take your heels out of his sides.

And then there is the bit. The same term "soft" can apply to this. Because, you rarely see an ad that says, "horse has hard mouth", it's safe to say that the horse will always have a soft mouth, no one EVER lies about this, ever. This is simple, the harder the mouth, the less chance you must stop. If you reach in his mouth and you feel very well built, Italian leather shoes on the side of this mouth where the bit sits, chances are that he's got a hard mouth. The benefit to this is, you won't have to worry about hurting him. The con is, you really won't be able to ride with your friends because you won't be able to stop. Another thing that connects to the bit is the turning capabilities. Most important question is, "does he?" I'd hate to be on the non-turning horse when he gets to the end of the arena. He may not turn immediately, and it may not concern you because you're already in love. Eventually, this will be kind of important, especially if you ever need to avoid a tree, fence, another rider, a slow-moving cat, a rose bush, a cactus, another person, or anything else that may not be able to get out of the way fast enough.

If you've moved on to trying him on the trail, you'll be confident that he'll be much better behaved, since he's been so good in the arena. Horses are always the same on the trail, so it shouldn't be a problem. Don't get me wrong, he may be great, which he should be since the ad said, "trail safe and bombproof." The first sign of a problem is seeing the whites of his eyes the minute the gate opens. If this happens, activate your parachute and jump. You'll want to test all the same buttons when you are out of the arena. Hopefully, they will all work just as well, even though there won't be a rail to keep you going in a circle. Pre-map the area in case it's a while before you can stop, turn, avoid obstacles or need a vehicle to pick you up when he does finally stop in the next county. Since this is the trail test, you should do everything you can to avoid coming across any potentially scary objects like; cats, lizards, white rocks, black rocks, a stick or a person standing someplace where they shouldn't. The seller said he's fine with everything but on this particular day, they've noticed he seems to be on "high alert", which is extremely abnormal for him. Oh, one more thing, don't forget to double check your cinch. Otherwise, you may have the same sequence of events, except you'll see everything from upside down, on the ground or from his side. This would be great fun for your trainer since trainers can also act as stunt doubles. If you do have your trainer with you for your test rides, I am guessing they will be ready with margaritas for everyone watching when you finally get off your prospective horse, Wilbur.

The final ride evaluation is getting off. Few people think this is important, but the exit is equally as important as getting on him and the ride itself. If you had to evacuate during the test ride itself, you should still evaluate how you dismounted. This is important because you may still think this is the perfect horse for you, so you will really need to make sure you can do the emergency dismount well. The best dismount for the unplanned exit is the fly, drop and roll. You don't fly off by choice but once you fly, you'll quickly realize you're going to drop and if you're lucky, you'll have time to roll instead of "splat". If it was a great ride, you should test the horse's tolerance. How many ways will he let you get off. Can you pull your feet out of the stirrups, hang like superman across his back and slide off like a world-famous gymnast? Maybe you can even slide off his backend. Maybe you've already slid off his back earlier when you couldn't stop him. If there is any question at all, landing while still standing is the number one choice. If he is witty, needs to impress his friends or just feels like testing you, he'll step off to the side as you dismount. If this happens, chances are that your foot will be caught in the stirrup and you'll wind up under him. He won't run though, he'll be too busy looking down at you laughing along with his friends and your trainer. The seller will say, "Wow!!!!! I've never seen him do that before." Your trainer will be happy to help correct that for a small training fee once you get him home.

Just a recap on the important points of the test ride:

- If he doesn't stop in the arena, odds are he won't stop on the trail.
- The cat sitting on the rail while you're in the arena is a friend, the same cat sitting on the rail when you leave the arena is going to kill him.
- The gate out of the arena is not the starting line for the horse race.

- If you can jump high, ride through unexpected side movements, handle the wind through your ears and flapping cheeks and fly faster than superman, you don't need brakes. If your trainer can do these, you still don't need brakes, your trainer will happily fix this for you, for a small fee.
- Always carry a parachute and 25 rolls of toilet paper, it makes the unexpected dismount a much softer landing.
- Always carry certified, organic carrots. If you do need to get him to stop, you can always reach into your pocket (while he gallops down the trail) and grab a carrot. The minute he smells it, he'll come skidding to a stop just long enough to grab the carrot from your hand before running off and leaving you in the dust.

Please note, some sellers are extremely conscientious of your safety, so they give Wilbur just a small shot of something to take the edge off. The seller will be happy to ride him for you. You'll see how safe he is, and you can't wait to get on him. Once you finally get him to walk at .0735 mph, you're comfortable taking him for a short ride on the trail. OMG!!!!! He's wonderful!!! A freight truck drove by, carrying a load of Harley's that were revving their engines while the truck used it's Jake break and Wilbur didn't even spook! Don't worry, you'll get the "Fresh" feeling when the drugs wear off about 2 weeks after you've brought him home, just past the "trial" period. This is the point when bomb-proof, husband safe Wilbur winds up in the tree because a cat walked by.

CHAPTER II- HE'S HOME

The test ride was great! He only took off 5 times, it only took you 28 minutes to stop him (but it got better each time) and your trainer has convinced you she can fix anything. Now it's time to really get to work. He's coming home, you get to unload him from the trailer. His stall is ready to go, you've made sure the arena has been sanitized so he can play without catching anything from any of the other horses, and you've spent $200 on different foods so you can figure out what he likes.

The Truth About Unloading

He's just arrived. You weren't there to see him load, but since the seller said he trailers perfectly, he must unload perfectly, and you are there to welcome him to his new home. I recommend a few things before even taking him out of the trailer:

- Un-tie him and have someone hold him while you open the trailer gate (if he's in a straight load or the last slant). Or, your trainer can tell you that it's okay to go ahead and open the door, no he won't try to jump out, he's still tied in. So, the door opens, and the rear end comes out, but the front does not. Since the first decision to keep him tied was so smart, it's time to make another one. You immediately go to the rear end and try to push Wilbur back into the trailer so you can get him untied. This leads to the dance which confirms Wilbur's description as "beautiful mover". You push forward on Wilbur's beautiful big rear end and Wilbur

26

lurches back. It's like the bad version of the "Boot Scoot Boogie". He is now pulling hard on the rope that won't let him out of the trailer. He swings his butt as you go flying into your trainer (you know, the one that caused this mess). Quickly you get up and try to push him back into the trailer, or forward, or sideways, or up to the sky; anything that will loosen the lead. As you give one last heave and ho, his line snaps and now you both go flying back together. You've just gotten up close and personal with his tail and his rear end (which appears to be perfectly healthy). Wilbur stands forward and mixes himself a margarita while you brush off your new horses very healthy poop and get his tail hair out of your mouth. Lesson, untie the lead line before letting him dance out of the trailer.

- Have a lot of carrots ready. You'll need these to either persuade him back into the trailer so you can untie him, feed him quickly, before he pulls the lead out of your hands while unloading and tries to run home, or get him to follow you to the stall you've just padded with 18 feet of shavings and a personal choice of other organic treats.
- Drop the window where his head is. Whisper sweet-nothings to him, talk "baby talk" and let him know you are ready to do whatever he wants. Oh, and un-tie him.
- Un-tie him (did I say that already?)

Getting Wilbur Settled

It's time to get him settled into his new digs. You've set them up just perfectly. You were very selective with his neighbors. You've got a gelding on one side and a mare on the other since you don't really know his "preference". Arabian geldings usually prefer boys.

27

You take him down and let him settle in. He happily starts munching away at his perfect appetizer of organics, takes a drink of the wonderful margarita you've made (with quality Tequila, of course), and promptly pees in his shavings. Your outraged, you've spent 5 hours spreading those shavings perfectly and now he stares you in the eyes, legs spread, thoroughly drenching your $20 per bag shavings. Think of it as his way to say thank you and "I am going to make your life hell and leave you financially drained."

After you're done staring at him in glee, for about 9 hours, it's time to take him back out and show him off around the ranch, but first he gets to go jump and roll in the pen. Everyone loves your magnificent new Wilbur. He's so well behaved! Just as you get him in the arena gate and before it has a chance to close, he's gone (taking part of the halter with him); running like a wild mustang, screaming for his friends and clearly making it abundantly obvious you won't be catching him anytime soon. Now everyone is really watching. Some have the look of "What the hell did you do?", some are in full blown laughter at "What the hell you just did", and some remembering that their horse did the same thing when he arrived. Finally, Wilbur has settled down enough for you to only have to run about 6 laps to catch him. You've gotten a great workout and he's ready to go to bed.

The next day starts with sunshine and smiles. You've got Wilbur and you can't wait to see him. He'll be waiting for you, his new "human". The moment you see him, you don't get what you were expecting. As we have all learned, peace between new horses doesn't happen overnight, and the war waits until we go to sleep. The panels are bent (on the mare's side so we now know what he doesn't like), there are about 20 new scratches and marks on him and his gelding neighbor is missing part of his mane. Wilbur has officially settled in to his new room.

Going Broke with Feed

Now it's time to figure out what he'll be eating besides organic carrots, apples and the occasional (pre-ride, custom blend) calming hay. Wilbur should start with whatever he ate at the old place, which was probably equine caviar and golden laced oats. You'll need to start weening him off this feed, so you can continue to support his other horse habits and apply any extra money toward your saddle costs. What kind of hay will he eat? How much will he eat? Will it be the same as his neighbors? Perhaps you should just throw the feed in between stalls so they can share. Any good owner knows the important addition to feed is the supplement. The supplements have everything you need for a horse to thrive. It's not about what's in the supplement; it's what the supplement will cost. Wilbur, like many horses, will like the most expensive one. This is probably the same one that is developed to enhance the performance of race horses. My recommendation is to buy one bag of everything with a feed bowl to go with each. Pour a little handful of each in a separate bowl and line them up. Don't even offer the really expensive stuff if you can't afford it. That's what he would like best and he won't be happy if you just tease him with it.

CHAPTER III- SAFETY IS WHAT SAFETY DOES

Before you get too comfortable, it's important to remember safety. This is very serious, and too many people get injured because they just don't pay attention. That said, there are some crazy things that happen when you take a moment to forget safety. There are some common safety issues that I see a lot, from positioning ourselves in the perfect position to receive a kick to feeding our fingers to the horses. Sometimes, we forget our BFF's are 1,000 lb. animals and wear our day to day clothing out there, sometimes this makes it too easy for Wilbur to get to bad places.

He Kicks, You Scream

A kick from a horse is not uncommon at all and it happens for enough reasons to write a separate book. In addition to the kick itself, there are about 3,000 ways to get kicked and about 5,000 places to get kicked. Some can make you look like Superman (or Superwoman). The famous safety error that I have seen a lot in my past years has been the infamous "walking behind the horse's rear end so he can kick you" error. Oh wait, I haven't only seen it, I did it and it landed me a torn thigh muscle and 15 stitches. I was lucky, I had a great doctor at the ER (not the horse). He was able to put in very strong thread, so I could ride that afternoon. There are different levels of this safety blunder and they range from "ouch my foot" to "I really wish I had a helmet on".

The best-case kick scenario is the "ouch my foot" scenario. Since you've had Wilbur a whole two days, you are already best buddies. This means you can do ANYTHING with him. There is no reason you shouldn't be able to walk out of nowhere and ask him to pick his foot up. Right! You give him a little tap on the thigh and gently ask him to lift his foot up for you. Oh, he does. He lifts it, tucks it and sets it down just as quickly. Except, when he sets it down, the ground is much softer for him. Now he's asking you, in horse language, why the ground is so much softer? Unfortunately, you can't really answer his question because you don't speak horse language and his foot is on yours from the half kick foot-land. And, like any perfect horse will do, he makes sure to lean on you because he wants to be closer to his new best friend. I forgot to add that he is "light to the touch", which was part of the ad. Softly, you push his rear end, so he'll move away from the pressure. Huh. Does, "light to the touch" mean push into pressure? At this moment in time it does, and Wilbur pushes right back, putting heavier pressure on your foot. Since your foot is now going numb and the pain is slipping away along with your blood flow, you ask your trainer to go pick up lunch and ask your friend to make you a very strong margarita. Now you're getting desperate. It's time to start negotiating. You make a deal with Wilbur; if he gets off your foot, you will feed him nothing but carrots, the special calming hay and organic apples for the rest of his life. Careful, he'll hold you to that promise and when he moves his foot off, he looks at you at once with a smile. Don't be fooled. If you don't keep your promise, your other foot will match.

The second rear end scenario is the warning kick. It's not really a warning because you didn't give him a warning when you walked up behind him and gave a love tap on his thigh. In return, he gave you one back. Luckily, he already loves you, so it was a light love tap. He only kicked you hard enough to make you scream out loud. Something like, "You son of a horse!!!!!" He smiles, and you walk away, limping and smiling but moving as fast as you can to get a strong liquid remedy. The warning kick can land anywhere but it won't be hard enough to break or pop anything. If he gets you in the chest, you won't even have to worry about replacing your implants.

The worst of the kicks is the angry Wilbur. Angry Wilbur means business and you're his business. Whether you surprise Wilbur or not, the angry Wilbur kicks with intent. What can create such an angry force? Well, you may have broken your promise the first time he stepped on your foot because you never fed him the organic apples, he needed to remind you that he doesn't like the color of his halter, he found you didn't let him test eat the expensive supplement, and the list goes on. Or, he found out you cheated by giving him over ripe apples that were genetically altered and not organic. If you are new to horses, I strongly recommend you wear a breast protector, steel tipped boots (oh wait, you returned those boots) and a helmet any time you're around Wilbur so you can protect yourself while you can learn how hard and why Wilbur can kick when you break your promises.

Wilbur may also happily present you with this type of kick if you hurt something while you're back there. Just a few tips to avoid this type of kick:

1) Don't use scissors, gardening sheers, or a sharp knife to clean his back feet. If you insist on using any of these tools, please use a Motocross face mask to protect your recently paid off nose job.
2) Don't use any of the above tools to clean off that extra future fertilizer around his tail. If you insist on this, please make sure you have your breast protector and knee pads on. The breast protector will protect your recently paid off automatic landing protection devises (aka breast implants).
3) Don't run up behind him with plastic bags tied all over your body.
4) Don't invite your trainer and her horse to see how symmetrical Wilbur's rear end is from close. Better yet,

don't stand between them when her horse is near sighted and really needs a close-up view.

5) Don't follow Wilbur in the round pen, chasing him with a whip while holding his tail so you can dirt ski (definition will be further defined later). This is a dual sword. The double barrel kick will ensure you'll need to buy stock in face protector's, chest protectors and even parachutes. Also, you'll drag uncontrollably behind your horse until the shock and pain subside enough for you to let go. The worst part about this scenario is, by the time you come to a complete stop, catch your breath, assess the skid marks, assess the broken face mask and let go of the hair still clutched in your hand; your audience (all the other horses and people at the ranch) will have had time to mix drinks, grab chairs and pick up chips and salsa so they can enjoy the full show.

I think I've made enough of a point on avoiding the kick. If you take anything away from this segment; either wear all of your protective gear or let your trainer do this. Or, just let Wilbur know you are there, promise him organic carrots and apples if he's good and don't break your promise. Horses know when promises are broken.

Don't Get a Bad Wrap

Another common safety hazard is the "wrap around" (WA). This is any line that is connected to your horse wrapped around any part of your body, thus making you two as one. Well shucks, you are already best friends and can read each other's minds, so you are as one. And when he is done dragging you around, you will still be connected as one. You can do the hand to lead, lead to waist, lead around ankle, and both hand pull. It will be like dancing the Cha-Cha with a 1,000-pound partner.

The most common WA (wrap around) is the hand to the lead. Whether you are taking him out of the stall, out of the pasture, out of the arena, out of the bar, or out for a walk, you find it's much easier to just wrap the lead line around your hand rather than try to coordinate carrying some long line that gets you all tangled up. No matter where you are taking Wilbur from and to, there really is only one outcome for this set up; the crash, drag and exfoliate. If you are wearing tennis shoes, you may be able to sprint alongside while he drags you. It's simple scenario; Wilbur decides he wants to go faster than you can, so he does (perhaps the happy drugs wore off) and since you are connected as one, you go with him. If you're lucky and in great shape, you can keep up with him for a bit. All the onlookers think you are jogging together. This will last until you get tired and he's still running. The other possibility is that you are taken by total surprise and you get yanked on your face at once, dragging behind him like a dirt-face-skier in tow. Or, you don't get caught by surprise and you see it coming but you can't get your hand out of the loop fast enough. The problem is that you're not in shape at all, completely uncoordinated and still a little light headed from the kick. Regardless of the previously mentioned above three, the outcome is usually the same; I have officially defined this as the "drop, drag and exfoliate". If you get dragged far enough, not only will you exfoliate your face, but the exfoliation will include part of your body as well, after your clothes have started tearing away. There is no doubt that the same audience as the arena incident will be there to watch. However, viewing might be a bit difficult because this time, you are speeding across the ranch.

If you really want to make an impression with your trainer and friends, go use the outhouse. The trick is to keep Wilbur just on the outside, with your hand wrapped in his lead from the inside. This is a critically timed trick because you really don't want him to run off until your pants are completely down to your ankles. Make sure the door will open when he turns into a race horse so the full effect of you and your bare rear end can be visible to the satellite in space. Better yet, that highly paid trainer runs at him with bags tied all over her body while you sit peacefully in your own private outhouse. I can't emphasize enough how important it is for that door to open when this happens. If you're able to latch it somehow, the outcome will be much different, and you'll really wish it had just been cleaned. Do I need to further clarify this? I could write a whole book just on this scenario.

Once in a great while, you may be feeling exceptionally intelligent and decide to wrap the lead line around your waist, tying it so it won't come loose. This is a great way to multitask and carry several items while leading your bomb-proof horse. If he does decide to move faster than you (odds are he does) you will want to make sure all the other things you're carrying are not breakable or are in protective cases. If you really want to ensure the greatest safety while leading Wilbur like this, just set up barriers built with very soft toilet paper, so you have a soft landing. Or, another recommendation is, just don't do it.

Barefoot but Not Beachbound

I am sure your trainer talked to you about your shoe choice and what shoes are safe to wear when you're around Wilbur. When you went to look at Wilbur, you wore your steel-tipped, brand new $768 riding boots. Now that Wilbur is home, you don't need to use those boots. After all, you are BFF's. You've returned the boots and added the $768 to your saddle fund. You can trust Wilbur because he stops within 500 feet of dragging you and he only kicks you twice a week. You know his every move, which means you have a lot of footwear choices. If it's warm, the best choice is barefoot. The dirt is always soft and there is nothing like feeling natural and free when you're with your horse. You can enjoy the benefits of being barefoot before you even get to your horse. The soft dirt warms your feet, you can feel nature between your toes. If you're lucky, the jagged rock or nail you step on won't pierce your foot, it will just really hurt for two days. And those are the benefits before you even get to your horse.

Once you get to your horse, the barefoot benefits really present themselves. Since Wilbur will be so happy to see you, he'll come trotting right up to you, waiting for you to put his halter on. Now, to protect your bare feet, you can stand back and lean forward, reaching out to put it on. Or, you can stand normal. Wilbur will drop his head for you, you'll get the halter on him, and you both will be ready to walk out of the stall. He politely walks right next to you, just like a dog, until you hear someone from far away bite into that organic apple. Remember the one you promised Wilbur? Unfortunately, he remembers you never fulfilled that promise so now he can get it from this person. He steps forward a bit quicker than you and you suddenly hear a "crunch". Well, you know no one is eating chips around you so it must be the sound of your friend eating that apple. Nope, can't be that because you just realized your foot won't move and you're feeling like someone just dropped a sledgehammer on it. You look down to see his foot on yours, it's like holding hands at the prom. The good thing is, you can see one of your toes is still attached. You're not sure about the others because you can't see them. You can also see a small part of your foot hanging out from the side of his hoof. If it wasn't attached and you couldn't feel the increasing screaming pain, you wouldn't recognize it because it's flat. At least your leg will still be attached to your heel because that's what you'll be walking with while in your cast, after plastic reconstructive toe surgery. By the way, you just used your "Buttocks Implant" funds for this medical emergency.

Another popular safety issue for footwear is the Tennis/running shoe. We'll call it the Nik-oy. As in nice and "oy" my foot. Although it may not hurt quite as bad as being barefoot, you'll still hear the crunch. (Also, there is an added benefit to using a running shoe, if you want to practice acrobatics, it's perfect since it will slide right through the stirrup when you're riding.) The tennis shoe is the gremlin that we think is safe and it's so comfortable it's hard to resist. In the horse world, the tennis shoe was built to trick you. It's the little gremlin that says, "your foot is covered, you don't need to worry about being stepped on". So, when you are out playing with Wilbur, you go on your happy go lucky way until you suddenly stop. You've stopped because Wilbur has just taken a turn to the left, landing his foot on your Nik-oy. This time you don't get to see your toes to make sure they're still there, you only feel and hear the crush. When this happens, I recommend you keep that shoe on until you've gotten a strong margarita and a doctor because when you take that shoe off, it will be 3 times larger than it was before. It's critical your feet are the same size when around horses because if they are uneven, you'll not only walk crooked, but you'll be crooked in the saddle and this will make it much easier to fall sideways when you forget to tighten the cinch. And that will cost you another $1,000 to be deducted from your saddle fund.

Those Ain't No Treats

If they don't get you with the kick or the step, they will get you with a bite. Usually you will get all three within a proximity of time from when you bring Wilbur home. I know this is coming as a surprise, but horses can lick without biting. Hmmm.. not most of the time. There is nothing like getting a kiss from your horse, right? There is no better way to teach Wilbur to kiss you than to use treats. You finally found those magical organic apples and you cut a little piece to lure Wilbur's face toward yours. Now that your foot has fully recovered and the road rash on your face has healed, you know Wilbur will be much more careful around you and there is no better way to improve the bond than a little kiss. As you hold up your fingers, carefully covering the apple, he reaches out to gently take the piece of apple from them. Since Wilbur is your BFF, he knows the difference between your fingers and the apple piece. Ya, okay, time to wake up. This isn't a fairy tale. When Wilbur reaches out for that organic treat, he thinks he's getting a salad; a piece of apple wrapped in 5 little organic pieces of carrots. Finally, your fulfilling your promise that you made when he stepped on your foot! When Wilbur reaches out for his treat, he reaches out for the whole salad, aka your hand. Turns out, the carrots are your fingers! Youzzzaaaa, good thing he was still holding on to your fingers when you tried to pull them away; otherwise you may have fallen, and he would have stepped on your bare feet. Remember the "release to pressure" training? It turns out that pushing Wilbur's nose while screaming into his ear does not apply to finger holding pressure release. You push and he holds on tighter. It's time to take serious action. You call for crowbars while you gently try to pry his teeth apart to get your fingers out. It is amazing how strong those jaws are. Finally, you get Wilbur to loosen his grip just enough to get your fingers out of his mouth. What is the outcome? Wilbur didn't get his carrots or apple (you still owe on that promise) and your fingers are black and blue where his teeth gently sat on them. Well, that was a onetime occurrence, you'll teach him to kiss without biting your nose or fingers off. It's going to be difficult to hold the margarita glass in that hand. Be careful, noses look a lot like pieces of sugar. If you have a cold, they also look like that special kind of hay that keeps him calm.

Biting fingers won't be Wilbur's only trick. He's smart and underestimating the bite factor may help you lose weight, since chunks may start coming off your body. I say "chunks" because treats are usually kept in pockets of clothing that are close to parts of your body, depending on the attire you wear and when he bites those parts, he'll take a "chunk". A lot of people wear the button-down shirts with the pockets over the chest. This is probably the area Wilbur learns about the quickest. These folks usually put the treats in those pockets. If you are a male, Wilbur will learn that a bump in that area means there is something in it for him. I recommend you don't ever let your girlfriend borrow that shirt when she's around Wilbur. If you are female, you've got a lot to protect. I don't know about you, but I paid for mine and I can't afford to pay for another set, especially when I need to buy another saddle. Wilbur will learn very quickly that bumps on the front taste good and he can get to them with or without those pockets.

For those who wear jeans, the treats are usually stuffed into the back or front pockets. Nothing like having a long orange thing sticking out of your pocket. Haven't you ever heard the saying, "Hey! Is that a carrot in your pocket or are you happy to see me?" Wilbur's version is, "Hay! That's an organic carrot in your pocket and it's for me, so I'll just grab it." Putting treats in your jeans is like playing chess with the doctor who wants to change your sex. Front pockets decide pitch of voice and important body parts. Wilbur doesn't learn to find treats in these pockets as quickly as the shirt pockets but once he does, you'll know it. *Anything* that makes it look like something is in those pockets will be appetizing to Wilbur, anything. Do I need to expand on this?

Finally, there are those beautiful nice tight stretch pants we all look so fabulous in. Everything is smooth, they have beautiful pockets on the sides, where Wilbur learns you hold the treats. Riding pants show everything, so it's not that hard to see when treats are in the pockets on the sides of your thighs.

This is why I refer to "chunks": if he goes for the chest, he'll get a breast; if he goes for the rear of the jean pocket, he'll get a chunk (in my case a bigger chunk); if he goes for the front pocket, perhaps size does matter; if he goes for the pocket that sits on the side of your thigh, he'll get a chunk. It's just important to remember that when you are breaking up those carrots and/or hiding those treats in different parts of your clothing, he's watching and learning. You may not think he's watching but he is and when you put something in that pocket instead of a treat, he'll know that, but he'll still take that chunk to teach you to never forget to put anything other than a treat in that pocket again.

CHAPTER IV- MAKING WILBUR PURDY

The next logical step for improving that great relationship is looking pretty. It's time to get yourself and Wilbur all your riding and groundwork gear. Before you know what to buy, you've got to make Wilbur pretty. You'll need at least 10 hours. But, you'll want to spend at least a little time before you ride or take him out to show off. There are so many steps to making sure you have a pretty horse; brushing, mane and tail, cleaning and polishing the feet and bath time, to name a few... You may only have time to do some and you may have the full 10 hours to do it all.

Brush, Spend, Brush, Spend

Brushing Wilbur will be what you do most often. You'll brush him before you do any groundwork. You'll brush him after you do groundwork. You'll brush him before you saddle him, even if you just finished brushing him from his groundwork. You'll brush him after you ride. You'll brush him again after you've ridden him, brushed him and let him roll. How dare Wilbur roll after you've brushed him so well. Don't think this will be it: it becomes an addiction. You might as well keep a medium and a stiff brush at his stall because you'll need (remember, it becomes an addiction) it when you see that Wilbur rolled in his pee shavings and has clumped pee dirt on his side. You will never want anyone to see Wilbur with a pee stain on his side.

You'll also have a great choice of brushes, even though you only need 3 (a nice soft one for his face, a good one for his mane and tail and a semi-stiff one for the rest of his body). Even though you only need three brushes, you'll want 10 brushes and 3 combs. The brushes will range from something so soft it really doesn't do anything except feel soft. This will be the prettiest brush and the brush that will be used the least, because it's so soft it doesn't clean any part of Wilbur's body. The stiffer brushes will be the ones that look like human brushes for long hair. They have a nice handle with stiff, wider set thistles that comb through a mane and tail easily. Here is another investment tip; you can usually buy these from the .99 cent store instead of the feed store for $24.00. This way you can add the difference back toward your savings for your future saddle. You will probably find that the brush you buy for Wilbur's mane and tail works great on breaking up the caked-on pee clumps, so you should buy a few of these. If you want to do a "double fisted" brush, you can put a stiffer brush in one hand and a slightly less stiff brush in the other hand, enabling you so you can brush Wilbur just like Wax On, Wax Off.

To Fly Away Mane or to Not Fly Away Mane

Wilbur's mane and tail will always need attention, sometimes more than other times. You'll find yourself using the .99 cent hair brush a lot for his mane and tail. It will be much easier to brush them out if you invest in a very expensive equine detangler and use at least half the bottle each time you brush them out. It will have to be an expensive one though, because anything less will pull out too much hair and just not make him shine enough. Since you're buying the detangler, you might as well buy the matching shampoo. Wilbur will need his mane and tail brushed when you notice it's not sitting perfectly, there are a few knots, after he's rolled (which is after you've already brushed him once), when it's really windy and it looks like someone stuck his hoof in an electrical socket and (I left the best for last), when you let him roll and he somehow got into

45

the brush, brought most of it back and allowed it to become hopelessly tangled in his tail. If you need to save more money for the perfect saddle, I would recommend just cutting both his mane and tail off because it's difficult to look at a tangled mane and tail. Just kidding, what would the other horses think!

Sparkling toes and Sauerkraut

There is a difference between cleaning and polishing Wilbur's feet. Cleaning them means getting under those things and getting all the gooey, nasty, poopy, dirty build up out from his hooves. Consider this his collection area. Like brushes, you'll have several choices of hoof picks. Since this mixed concoction will be hard as a rock by the time you get to it, you'll want a hoof pick that doesn't bend. You'll need to be prepared though, as soon as you get through the hard stuff, you'll get to the soft stuff and the hoof pick moves much faster then you're prepared for. Initially, you'll either fall forward with your face landing squarely in the stuff you just got out of his foot, or you'll give yourself a nasal enema with the hoof pick because someone told you to clean the feet by having the hoof pick come toward you instead of away; maybe your trainer. Some metal hoof picks have built in magnets, so they hang on their own. These are great, especially when Wilbur has shoes. It's okay to not clean Wilbur's feet for a bit. Just remember, the stuff inside between the hoof and the frog is a collection of poop, hay, more poop and clay. The longer you go between cleaning, the more that stuff will smell like rotten sauerkraut. I think it's called "Kimchi". If you go about a week, you can collect it and can it. I'm sure it's a delicacy someplace in the world. You know you're doing a good job when he farts while you're cleaning his back feet.

Polishing Wilbur's feet is a preference of how shiny you really want his feet to be. If you want to add some bling to match your plans for a bling halter, they even have sparkles. If you want a shiny rustic look, you can polish his feet and throw dirt on them while the polish is still wet.

You Can Never Over-bubble

And finally, there is bath time, the most fun of all grooming exercises. Since you are a considerate owner who doesn't want Wilbur to get cold, you'll only be bathing him when it's warm. I must warn you, if you decide to wash Wilbur when it's cold and he must be in the cold while he dries, he'll remember, and you'll get to feel the angry kick later, even if you make up for it with organic apples. It's warm, it's sunny and Wilbur has a big giant stain on the side of him. You've used the stiff brush, the semi stiff brush, the soft brush and the mane/tail brush but the stain is still there. You bought the high-grade shampoo that matches the high grade detangler, so you are ready to rock-n-roll. Brakes please.... You're only ready to go if you also bought the Sparkle and Shine post shampoo rinse and the 27 scrubbing brushes that you'll use for round one bath. You'll soak him well, he'll only try to kick you when you start using the full strength of the hose aimed right at his face. Suds him up well, use at least 2/3 of the expensive shampoo. Make sure you have your deep-toothed bath, flexible, bacteria resistant, iTune friendly hand gloves. When he's engulfed in white bubbles (you'll know when to stop when you can't see his body anymore), rinse. If you want to conserve and share the costs of the shampoo, have a friend's horse stand next to you so the bubbles blow onto him as you rinse. While you are rinsing, you can use the same gloves to make sure you can get the shampoo mostly out. You don't

47

have to get the shampoo all the way out because the stains won't disappear, so you'll have to suds up again, using what you have left of your top-quality expensive shampoo. Once you rinse the second time, you'll want to make sure the shampoo is completely out. The stains will still be there, but the shampoo will be gone so that's as good as its going to get. To get all the water out, you can use a car squeegee or a horse squeegee. The horse squeegee will work much better and it will only be about $ 10more. The horse squeegee is great. You should buy 20 of them because there are so many other uses, including hitting your trainer when they've told you that Wilbur doesn't really need a bath. Once you're done bathing him, don't forget to brush him. After you've brushed him, turn him out into a soft pen so he can roll and you can start the process all over again.

CHAPTER V- GET YOUR REAR IN GEAR AND GET YOUR GEAR

Before you're ready to start working with Wilbur, you need to make sure you've got all your gear set up. There are many choices for picking out your gear, like picking out the perfect outfit for yourself, from your undergarments to the last lace on your new paddock boots. You'll need your ground work gear and your riding gear. This segment could get a bit lengthy since each riding discipline calls out for different equipment. We're not going to get that detailed; after all, you're just getting started with Wilbur. You won't know if you want to be a professional trainer or jumper for at least 5 months. The groundwork gear is what you need to do all your groundwork with Wilbur while you work to improve that "already perfect" relationship all before you jump into the saddle. You can get out of the store without breaking your wallet for this gear since there aren't many pieces. The second round of gear is your riding gear. Like I said, there are a lot of choices when picking out your gear, usually they are based on what type of riding you'll be doing. However, even though there may be variances based on the discipline, you still need a bridle, reins, a bit (or not), a saddle pad, and a saddle.

Your Everything Stuff

The most important gear choice you need to make, no matter how you ride, is your halter. This will define who you are and who your horse is. It doesn't matter what sex your horse is when choosing your halter. It's the statement that matters. How proud are you? In all my years of experience, it seems to be that a rider really wants to make a much louder statement in the beginning. I totally agree. There are so many ways to choose that perfect halter. You should have made this decision the minute you picked out Wilbur, because you knew it would fit his personality. Remember, no matter what your halter choice is, you always need to make sure the lead line matches. Why is a halter so very important for every aspect of handling Wilbur? Well, I'll let you do the experiment: lead him out of his stall, to the arena, to the tie rail or on a nice walk without it, he won't be there when you turn around to pet him. At least you won't get tangled.

The most common halter is the Nylon halter. It has simple snaps and a variety of colors to choose from. This one style of halter can offer you endless choices of how easily you really do want Wilbur to be seen. You can even buy multiple halters in different colors, so you can match Wilbur's mood or outfit for that day. Black, grey, standard single colors, all the colors of the rainbow, neon green with large yellow and blue polka-dots, glow in the dark, and sparkly (bling) are all choices you have. If you go for the loud colors, you should buy two or three, so you have replacements when the color starts to fade.

The rope halter is another choice and very popular these days. It has "pressure points" to help your horse understand what you want from him. This is a great way to show the world, "Hey, I can do more with less, but with a little more in the areas that there is a little less, so I have to ask less." Since this style of halter has become so popular, they've even started making these in multiple colors as well. Sadly, you don't get the cool unique patterns or bling, but you can get rainbow.

Oh, and then there is the Leather Halter, the regal of the regal. This halter says, "Money and top quality, pure organic feed only." The Leather halter is not kept out in the elements. It is conditioned regularly, it is soothed in the evening with a custom lavender blend of leather lotion. This is the halter you should use when presenting Wilbur for royalty. The leather halter does not come in multiple colors, that is beneath it. But, you can add bling. You can add sequins, custom stitching, Wilbur's name on one side, "You're the Best" across the nose bridge, and "Horse Ever" on the other side, just to make sure everyone knows how you feel about Wilbur. You can even get a large noseband, so you have more room to add his name, stitching or bling. Personally, I like to add the name in case I forget it while I am leading him. This can be an inexpensive choice. Just buy a used one from the last person who had a regal horse. You can change the name on the nose band or change Wilbur's name to match what's already on the noseband.

Another important piece of gear for ground and saddle work is the glove, as in the gloves you wear on your hands. Some people wear them, and some don't, but they are good to have around for a variety of reasons. I do not recommend buying used gloves. I recommend buying only new gloves and I recommend buying in bulk whatever brand you like the best because you will always be buying them. As a matter of fact, I would also recommend you invest in a nice container to hold your gloves because you'll always be losing them, they'll always be tearing, you will be missing sets and you'll always be buying at least 3 sets of your favorites plus 2 sets of the new magenta floral lace style they just came out with. Take comfort in knowing that no matter how many extra sets of gloves you may have, you will always find a set missing when you need them the most. This is my investment tip for you.

Hitting the Ground with the Groundwork Gear

There is basic equipment you'll want to have to work Wilbur on the ground. It's not much and often you can borrow it, or even buy it used so you can continue your feeble attempt to help your saddle fund. First, it's important to understand why you need gear for groundwork and what ground work is. Groundwork is the key element to ensuring your horse understands what you want from him, how you're going to ask for it, understands the native tongue in which you speak, can read your body language and look into your eyes to develop that strong sense of ESP you'll expect him to have. The goal for groundwork is, "Think it and he will do it." Groundwork is all the work you do with your horse from the ground. This includes driving, lunging, sensory and more. The most important reason for groundwork, besides setting up the strong eye contact ESP connection, is to learn about the hardness or softness of the ground when working with your horse. If you don't learn now, it will be a lot worse when you learn from the saddle.

The lunge line is an excellent tool to use for any type of groundwork since you can make it short or long. You can use it to work your horse in circles at different speeds in or out of an arena. Most trainers have at least 29 to 200 lunge lines in various lengths, so this is an item you may be able to borrow or buy cheap. Although some people believe in using a long lead line to do their groundwork, many people really like the lunge lines. It gives you more flexibility. Lunge lines come with multiple choices:

- Length: Your lunge line length can vary from 13 feet to 50 feet. You should figure out the desired length of your lunge line by how badly you want to get tangled up. The longer the lunge line, the more room you can give your horse to work around you. When you have a long lunge line and you draw your horse in, you get the additional benefit of circling with your horse while the extra length of the lunge line starts circling around your feet as you follow your horse. The longer the lunge line, the more loops get around your legs while you run the shorter line. Personally, I like a 30-foot line. This is just long enough to give my perfect horse room to perform all his movements and get enough speed to drag me off when he decides to stop lunging around me and start bucking down the arena. If I am using the full length of the lunge line, I'll be able to let go and watch him as he turns into a rodeo horse. If I am only using part of the length, I like to make sure I land on my back when I realize the extra lunge line is tangled around my feet and I am dragging behind him. Don't worry, you'll be far enough away to avoid the double barrel kick we discussed earlier. There is also the 50-foot option. You don't see these very often anymore, but they are still out there. Truthfully, I am not even sure of their purpose. I think they must have been developed by a rodeo clown because I've rarely seen someone use one of these without getting completely tangled up while lunging. I think you get the idea; longer=more room to go faster and more opportunity for some good old fashion fun dragging.

- Material: Not a lot of people think the kind of material used for a lunge line is important. This is an important choice for the lead line as well but it's very important for the lunge line. One would think this is a simple choice: cotton, poly, or rope (material?????). How tough do you want to be? If you want that "I can handle anything" type of tough, I recommend you go for the ropers rope. It's a stiff braided nylon rope that you don't need to connect as a lunge line if you don't want. You'll just swing it over and around your head screaming, "Yahoooo Wilbur, look me in the eye while I swing this rope at you." Wilbur will run around you in circles while you unknowingly get yourself tangled up and find yourself constantly jumping out of the tangled mess. The positive to this choice is that you usually won't find yourself getting dragged across the arena since it's not usually attached. Unless you unintentionally rope his head while swinging it over yours. That may take him by surprise. If you're not tangled up, he'll just leave without you. If you are tangled up, you'll go with him and everyone else will be screaming, "Yahoooo Wilbur". Nylon is always a good choice, especially if you don't want to wear gloves. Nylon is slick with so many benefits. That's why it's the easiest material to find for lunge lines. The best way to test this material to see if you like it is to lunge someone else's horse (because Wilbur is so good you won't get the result you need for this exercise) that really wants to go in fast circles around you and possibly just as fast away from you. Next, make sure you're not tangled and send your friends horse out to lunge. Make sure you hold on with both hands, so you can get the complete benefit of the Nylon experience. Once he starts to build momentum and pull you, the first thing you'll notice is an odd scent. It will be reminiscent of a campfire; soft scent of just adding a touch of fluid to the logs and getting that first aroma of the smoke. The second thing you'll notice is the actual smoke. This may be confusing for a moment because you're not actually camping. Once you realize the smell and vision of the smoke are connected to the area where your hands connect to the lunge line, it will all come together. And finally, there is cotton. Good ol' cuddly cotton. While you can still get the burn effect (to a much lesser degree), it's a fresher scent and doesn't leave nearly the deep grooves in your hands that Nylon does. Cotton can also stretch. This may be a good thing; if you need a little bit of time to get yourself untangled when you realize your horse is leaving, that stretch may give you a chance to get one foot out of the loop before he takes off. While cotton is nice and soft, it can unravel at the ends (either the snap end or the holding end). If you see it happening, you can let go before it breaks off and you go flying back while Wilbur goes running off. On a good note, you won't be getting dragged. On a bad note, Wilbur won't even have the line attached.

- The snap: This is how you will connect your horse to that lunge line. There are so many choices that it almost takes an evening of margaritas with Wilbur to decide which is best. There is the standard stainless-steel snap that that has a little lever to pull the snap open and closed. The lead is usually looped on so it's secure. This is the most common connection. This is a strong Pro: Wilbur may not have to run for very long before the snap snaps and you're not getting dragged behind him. There is also the carabiner clip type of attachment. You'll often see the lunge line looped into this and there is one piece that folds in, allowing it to open and close onto the halter. This is a solid piece of metal. It is made for the brawny tough horse or the handler that never wants the snap to break off when the horse is dragging you down the rail of the arena. This clip is also good for an emergency. When it needs to come off quickly, you'll find that it's that much more difficult to push the holder in and get it off the halter.
- The Lunge whip: is the whip that tells the horse go forward or backward or off into the sunset, depending on how you use it and what you're tangled on. This is the whip that is used for the ground, not to be confused with the whip that is used in the saddle. These whips come in many lengths. They also help define what kind of statement you want to make. Although the colors are slightly limited, some do come brighter than others. There is the longer whip which can reach the horse no matter how far away he is. This whip has great "snap and pop". It can be heard from across the ranch, spook the horses on the other side of the hill, and wake up the people in the neighboring county. Funny thing is; although everyone else will know it's there, Wilbur may just stand and look at you. Probably because he's waiting for your ESP signal. This whip has some dangerous traits. It's long, if you don't use it properly you'll find yourself with a

lot of whip marks on your backside before you're ever able to use it to move Wilbur. The longer it is, the more it hurts when it lands on you. And when it lands on you, the horses on the other side of the ranch will still spook, except it will be from your screaming. Once you've realized how badly it hurts, you'll be extremely careful when you learn how to aim it. The goal is to snap it behind Wilbur, but often it may either hit Wilbur on the rear or accidentally get tangled on his back leg. The rear snap may not be as bad, Wilbur will be startled but he will happily (and very quickly) go from a walk to a jump and full run around you. Let's hope you're not tangled up in the lunge line. The scarier thought is accidentally getting it tangled around his back leg. You'll have a moment to think on this one before Wilbur takes off. He'll probably look down at his leg and look at you in disbelief that his new love has just done this to him. That's when the ears will go back, his eyes will squint and turn into fire. You'll clearly hear him say, "Oh ya, I'll show you who oversees this whip", just before he takes off with it still attached. This is when you'll find out how smart Wilbur really is because he'll manage to aim the hard end of the whip right at your new nose job, so it snaps you before he runs off with lunge line and whip attached. The safer choice is the shorter whip that almost reaches Wilbur but doesn't touch him. This whip will also hit you in the back instead of the rear end while you learn to use it. Since Wilbur is so intelligent and you've connected on such a deep level, it won't be long before he realizes one of two things: 1) The whip won't really touch him when you crack it, so he'll stand there looking at you. He'll make you promise to feed him organic carrots and apples to move so you're not embarrassed in front of the margarita drinking crowd; or 2) you'll have to be close enough to him to make contact if you need. In this case, you better hope you've learned how to

57

use the lunge line correctly and how to get untangled quickly because, when he does feel the crack, he'll go forward and so will you.

The Saddle and What?

Now it's time to move on to Wilbur's riding gear. And you thought the ground work gear was confusing. Let's start from the head and move back to the tail. The headstall connects to the bit, the bit and headstall become the bridle, the bridle connects to the reins and the reins decide how fast you can't stop or turn. The saddle sits on top of the pad, which sits on top of the horse and you hope the saddle stays in place with the cinch. There is an additional section about extra gear, but these are the basics.

The bridle is the beautiful and possible safety piece that will be the controlling factor between you and Wilbur when you run the mountains, jump the fences (on purpose or accident), or gallop the arena. You know he can do this because he did it when you test rode him. Now, you've already learned what doesn't stop Wilbur, so you don't want to use what you used when you test rode him. There are two parts to the bridle: The headgear (we'll call it the headstall) and the bit (or not). This is another area I think they should have specialty stores for because there are way too many choices. When the headstall and bit are combined, they become the bridle. The headstall alone has multiple wonderful features to choose from.

The most common headstall is leather. The most common headstall style goes behind both ears with a browband (that thing that makes a horse look like a hippie) and connects to the bit. This is a simple piece. There is usually a throatlatch that goes under the cheek from the ears. Throatlatch straps are very important because this is what keeps your bridle on when Wilbur accidentally takes you through that thick brush that catches in the top of this bridle. This is not the place to try bridle-less riding. There is also single ear, double ear, pierced ear, and cover your ear choices. Each of these choices just makes it more difficult to put on because you need to remember what goes where. It's too easy to confuse one of the double ear pieces with the bit and wind up using the bit as the over the ear piece. I think I just confused myself. As with any piece of good leather, you can always add bling, sparkle and words. Another strong point to using leather is that you can stitch his name on the noseband in case you forget it. If you choose leather, you'll need to care for it like your leather halter by giving it a weekly massage with the, "I'm so expensive", lavender based leather conditioner.

Biothane is a mystical, magical, flexible, and colorful material that is easy to take care of and easy to see if you get lost in a deep canyon. It's washing machine safe. This material is what you want when you want your bridle to match the loud colors of your halter. Nothing says perfect like purple, blue and gold all over your horse's head. This strong material screams, "I want to make a statement and make sure the men on Mars can see me." It's super easy to clean, just throw it in the dishwasher with your fine china. And it's strong. If you are lucky enough to have Wilbur rear up on you while in the trees, you will both still be hanging when help arrives. If this does happen, you will owe Wilbur new colors and a barrel full of organic apples, after you've recovered from the pulled muscles of trying to hang on. And you will be hungover from drinking too many margaritas to dull the pulled muscles.

Rope headstalls come in all shapes and sizes. Rope headstalls are like visiting the candy factory. They can be twisted with multiple colors, braided, single material, with added features like feathers, fishhooks, earrings. They can be any color of the rainbow or all the colors of the rainbow. When you're done riding, you can even use these to add as decoration for yourself because they are so pliable. And because these are so pliable, there is a lot more you can do. They slip off extra easy and because they bend, you won't be able to fix it before Wilbur realizes it's off. Another thing to watch with a rope headstall is the lack of strength of the material itself. It's rope, not leather. When rope gets pulled, rope pulls apart. Don't plan on this type of headstall lasting for a very long. It will be pretty while it's together, but it will be ugly when it decides to fall apart. When it decides not to be "together", things will unravel (get it?) quickly for both the rope and your ride. A good choice if you want to use this type of headstall is to buy them like you purchase your gloves. Get a container and buy two every time you find new colors and styles you want.

It's just amazing that this doesn't even scratch the surface of headstalls, but I'd like to go ride when I'm done writing this book, so let's move on to bits. To bit or not to bit, that is the question. No, you won't get the answer, bit (I mean but) you will get lots of choices. Again, let's look at basic bit styles:

Snaffle bits are basically a simple style with a mouthpiece that bends in the mouth and is connected to a variety of oddly shaped sides. The reins connect directly to the bit. These bits can be thick, thin, twisted, have candy in the center, have permanent organic apple flavoring in the center or taste like sweet metal (what makes metal sweet anyway?). Some say this is a lower level bit that should be used for training. Others say it's too much metal. Trust me, you'll hear both. What matters is what's comfortable for Wilbur. I would buy a few, stick each one in Wilbur's mouth and ask him what feels the best. It is important to remember that snaffle bits bend in the middle, that means "bends over the tongue" and means much more to Wilbur than you. It will mean a lot to you when you accidentally twist the bit in Wilbur's mouth, catching his tongue and twisting that into a piece of licorice. It won't be the good tasting licorice either. You'll know this has happened when Wilbur suddenly becomes a flying, bucking bull like he did on the trial ride. His head will be tossing like he's rocking out to a metal band and you'll be tossing with him. Oh wait, maybe this is the bit you tried him in. If you use this type of bit, make sure you attach it untwisted before putting it into his mouth.

With Snaffle bits, you will hold one rein in each hand, turning with direct "pull" pressure. Hand goes left and you'll pull Wilbur's head left. Hopefully the rest of Wilbur's body will follow this time since it didn't during the trial ride. During the trial ride, Wilbur's head went left but his body kept straight, which is why they also described him as "athletic". This direct pressure will also affect the up and down of Wilbur's head and next movement. Envision this: when Wilbur takes off with you, left hand pulls up, back and out as if you are waving at an airplane. Wilbur starts to respond by lifting his head, pulling it to the left and appears to be reaching around to bite your toe. And, just when you realize he can reach your toe, your right hand pulls the right rein straight up. Wilbur's nose just got higher than his ears, which are flat back against his head (this is the middle finger of horse language). Wilbur had forgiven you for breaking your bribe apple promise, but now you're messing with his mouth that enjoys every bite of the $30 carrots you feed him and he's not going to take that. He'll have enough of your waving hands and his head will drop down as he pulls the reins from you. Your hands will be in the same place, like holding the lights that guide the planes in, but you'll be riding the full speed Wilbur instead of lovely Wilbur. There will be laughter, margaritas and lots of viewers for this event while you eventually land someplace other than near Wilbur with your hands in the exact same position.

The Curb bit is a leverage bit and adds shanks that attach your reins to. Take the choice of the snaffle bit and add 19 more choices. The Curb has different levels of upward curve in the mouth and has different sized shanks (the sides the reins attach to). It's really a simple process: the higher the curb angles the more it hits Wilbur's mouth. The longer the shank, the more the curb piece hits Wilbur's mouth when you pull the reins. For some reason, many people who ride in this type of gear feel that the higher the curb and longer the shank, the better the horse is and has a softer mouth. If you want something that says, "I am the rock! Wilbur is the prettiest horse in the world", you'll want a high-port, long shanked, sterling silver with custom engraved shanks. Who cares where your hands are because everyone will be looking at the ultimate mouthpiece that screams, "Wilbur rocks". Tip, don't use this bit with the synthetic headstalls. It will be like combining plaid and flannel with bright pink and mustard yellow.

This type of bit uses <u>soft</u> neck pressure. If you use this bit, you hold the reins with one hand and gently lay the outside rein (the one you want to turn him away from) over his neck and he moves off it like a 7-year-old ballerina. With this type of bit, the goal is to have Wilbur's head and neck almost parallel to his back and his nose slightly in, only slightly touching his chest. If you want to encourage this head position, put a piece of carrot in the front of your breast collar so he can reach down for it when he's dropping his head to the point of almost hitting his knee. You won't go far since he's busy trying to get the carrot, but he'll look pretty. Since Wilbur proved he wasn't "soft" during the trial ride, there is no way he's going to be soft with this type of gear. I'm sure your trainer can fix this for only about $500. With this type of set up, you'll have a different outcome when he takes off and you pull back. The actions will be as follows: Wilbur has had enough of you, so he's headed south, back to pee in his shavings. You respond by "lightly" laying the outside rein across his neck to turn him off the pressure. Remember, he's been trained to be light with pressure and you've already learned that wasn't the case when he stepped on your foot. Since you are resisting Wilbur's request and quickly learning that soft pressure isn't working, you revert to the snaffle rein position and hope for the best outcome. The audience saved the appetizers and drinks from last time, so they've had a chance to get a second round during this series of events. This movement will have a swift outcome, he'll drop his head and come to a complete stop in 7 seconds at which point you'll promptly fly over his neck, landing on your back only to see him looking down at you. He'll be laughing at you, but you won't hear it over the laughter of the audience around the arena.

If you want to show the world that Wilbur needs nothing in his mouth, go bit-less. There are lots of choices, again. In a nutshell, you pull the reins from the side (like a snaffle but no mouthpiece). Or you can use a set up where the reins are tied beneath Wilbur's chin, a bosal. With either of these set ups, the pressure is across the nose instead of coming from the mouth. The message for the horse that can ride in this set up is that he's so soft he doesn't need a bit. Sometimes it means the earlier owner couldn't stop him when he wore a bit so why keep trying and just hope for the best. If Wilbur does take off with this set up, you'll have the choice of flying sideways or over his head because he can move in any direction he wants. You'll be given the added choice of doing a double somersault off his back, as well, since he'll be able to start and run so fast.

Since you've picked the perfect headstall and bit, you officially have your complete bridle! You are hopeful that you can now control Wilbur. That said, the next step is to stay on so you can control Wilbur. While there is the possibility of riding bareback, which we'll touch on later, the saddle choices usually come next. Cover your wallet's ears, this is going to be painful.

Before you even put your saddle on, you'll need a saddle pad. The saddle pad is usually shaped to match the style of the saddle, so your biggest variances are the type of material you'll choose and some custom options (because just the type of material would make it way too easy). Material choices are usually wool, cotton, synthetic and neoprene. Sometimes you can do a pad under a pad. Sometimes you can add trim, you know the pretty fluffy edges that catch all the weeds on the trail? Some pads even come with little enhancements to help the saddles fit better.

The most common pad is the wool pad. It's natural, easy to clean, pulls the heat from the horse's back, and is easiest to find. The wool pad also helps teach you about time management. It can be a stiffer pad. This means that when you put it on the horses back it will sit straight across, not droop or settle in on the middle of his back. You put it on, make sure it's properly centered and notice it's not touching the middle of his back. It's stiff so it doesn't drape. Hmmm. The remedy to this is to go to the middle of Wilbur's back and push down so the pad settles evenly. Easy fix and you let go, pad goes back up, now above the middle of his back again. Easy fix and you push it down in the middle again. This time you're prepared, and you've grabbed yourself a cocktail, so you can stand holding the pad down with one hand and the drink in the other, leaning on it like that's exactly what you mean to be doing. Since this pad thickness can range from .25" to 1", the amount of time you'll have to spend standing there will vary. So, I suggest you get a pre-mixed container of margaritas in case you need to pour yourself another while you hold the saddle over the pad on Wilbur's back. Some people who use this pad put the saddle on, hoping the pad will just push down when the saddle is set on his back. The cowboys make it look so very easy. Throw on the ol' saddle pad, throw on the ol' saddle and you're done. Anyone who doesn't have a raspy voice can't do this in one simple step. For us novices (any non-trainers who've been riding for under 30 years), it takes a bit more than that. The process is usually:

- Put saddle pad on horse's back.
- Spend at least 20 minutes pushing it back, pulling it forward, and slightly pushing it back again. Find the perfect spot to

push it back down to and hold in place for a few minutes before putting the saddle on.

- Grab your saddle and throw it on Wilbur's back. As it lands, pad pushes back, under the saddle so the front of the pad has disappeared, but the back of the pad nicely sits just next to his tail. If you like this thought, you can do this instead of having a low pommel and high cantle since it will totally lift the saddle at the back.

- Pull saddle and pad off. You won't intend to do this, but the pad has become buddy sour to the saddle and they must go together. The pad conveniently drops on the ground while you set your saddle down.

- Put saddle pad back on his back, except this time you set up far up on his neck, so it doesn't slide back. Grab the saddle and put it on the pad just as high on his neck (about 1" behind the ears that are flat on Wilbur's head). Push both saddle and pad back until you feel the "soft spot", the perfect spot where the saddle should land. Slide, slide, slide.. oops you slid .048" too far and the pad kept going while the saddle stopped. Pad landing in same position as it did before.

- Repeat above steps 9 times.

The Neoprene saddle pad is somewhat new to the horse world. It's the surfers pad. It's advertised to "keep the saddle in place" when you ride, it doesn't absorb moisture and it's easy to clean. Great benefit, it also keeps the saddle in place when you ride no matter where that place is. Now, before you decide on this type of pad, it's important to assess how pads do what they claim to do. This is just a simple science formula; the horse has hair that goes in a certain direction and you want everything moving in that same direction. When you pull things against this direction, the result is an angry horse and we've already talked about what angry horses can do. You know this because you've given up on trying to pull the original wool pad against the hair since Wilbur kicked you each time you did this. For it to stay in place, it must stick to something. The question is what? Have you ever played with sticky glue? Again, this type of pad is pliable, it bends easily when the saddle is put over it. This makes it appear to be the perfect pad. Once the saddle is set in place, you are ready to cinch up and get on. No slipping there. Saddle didn't even turn sideways this time. Off you go onto the wild. ?????????????????????????? Now it's starting to make sense, the saddle hasn't slipped at all, but Wilbur would have already dumped you if you weren't in the "U" saddle with a nice high port, long shanked bit. It only happens when you go down a hill. I wonder why? The saddle really hasn't slipped. Also, oddly, the inside of your thighs have become completely saturated. There is so much sweat dripping off Wilbur's sides that you can start your own water desalinization plant and help resolve world thirst. Once you get the saddle and pad off his back, there is a dry area just around the shoulders that is the exact image of a special finger on your hand. (Some may not get this, but I'll let someone else explain that one.) On a good note, this pad will still be on Wilbur's back when he moves to the right as you try to put the saddle on and he takes off down the barn aisles. This pad will also make it clear where the saddle doesn't fit. And this pad is versatile. In between using it to ride with, you can roll it up and use it as a pillow for those nights when Wilbur has dumped you on the trail and it's too dark to walk home. If this happens, you'll get another benefit, the pad will be so smelly that the wild animals won't want to come near you.

Fleece saddle pads have become very popular. They are easy to handle and easy to clean. Better yet, they have so many color choices. If you took my advice to buy 1 of every color halter and biothane headstall, I recommend you do the same for the fleece saddle pad. It's just not right if they don't match. The fleece saddle pad has a few great benefits. They are so soft you can almost use them as a pillow for yourself. Just watch Wilbur's face when it's on his back. He'll gently close his eyes and drop his head knowing a little cloud of fluff is about to be set on him. And then he'll wake up when he realizes there isn't that much fluff between his back and the saddle. Fuzzy in the start, flat when they finish. This shouldn't be much of a problem if your saddle fits. If your custom saddle maker forgot to tell you that he didn't take the nails out of the bottom of this saddle, you'll find out when you go to ride Wilbur with the nice, soft, fluffy, fleece pad.

The saddle is the most important and expensive choice you'll make for Wilbur. Do not have any plastic surgery, eat out for dinner, buy your loved one an expensive toy, buy a new car or buy anything over $5.00. You'll need every cent possible to invest in your perfect saddle(s). Saddle prices range far and wide. Saddles are built for different purposes, but ultimately, they are the thing you try to keep your rear in while riding your horse. All saddles have similar components: the thing you sit in, the piece you sit on, something that curves up in the front (pommel), something that curves up in the back(cantle) and the strap(s) that hold the saddle on (cinch). Although they have several added choices, these are the basics no matter what design saddle you choose. I say "saddle" in singular form but I jest. I have yet to get away with trying to buy just one saddle.

Setting a true saddle budget is a simple calculation:

Saddle broke Investment calculations:

	$1,000	From your savings
Starting budget	$768	Steel tipped boot return
	$23	From money you saved on brushes
Total Money that you're ready to spend	$1,791	
Saddle #1	-$5,000	A bit more than you expected but it's really pretty
New Balance available	-$3,209	Turned out it didn't fit, you found out when Wilbur dumped you and you saw the open wound on his shoulder so now you must sell it.
Sell saddle #1	$500	You found out you were over charged, a lot. This was even high.
New balance available	-$2,709	
Hire custom saddle maker	-$1,000	
New custom saddle #2	-$3,000	You can ride bareback while you wait.
New balance available	-$6,709	
Sell Saddle #2	$1,000	You swear you never said seat size 12
		(that's a child's size!). At least you got a bit more because it was custom made.
New balance available	-$5,709	
Saddle # 3	-$3,500	It's perfect, Wilbur loves it, you love it. Until you go out for more than 1/2 hour and realize, it turns sideways costing you a trip to the ER (not the horse).
Emergency Room	-$2,000	
** No recoup on saddle because it's still somewhere in some bushes.		
New balance available	-$11,209	

You are officially in the hole $11,209. You'd be in the hole for more if you hadn't returned those boots and saved that money on your brushes. I'll bet your glad you didn't opt for takeout last night, as you just saved $15.00 toward these expenses. At this point, you get a second job and temporarily give up buying a saddle. You'll ride bareback until you can afford one again.

Now that you've worked 3 jobs, one being illegal but makes the most money, you are officially ready to start the search again. You've done all the research and truly know the choices you have now. Let's look at them.

They say the deeper the saddle, the easier it will be to stay on. I suggest you start with a saddle that is the true shape of a "U". U'll go nowhere when Wilbur goes south, north, east or west. I've never really seen a saddle with this deep of a seat, but I am sure a custom saddle maker would be happy to make it for you for only $10,000. That's almost what you'll spend on shavings each month. The pommel and cantle will decide how deep of a seat you have on your saddle. The shallower the saddle, the easier you fly. It's like a hammock, one good swing and you're off. A shallow saddle gives you a lot of flexibility to move in several directions. Not only can you easily go side to side (especially if the cinch has become loose) but you can also practice the "forward summersault, eye contact and hold maneuver", as well as the "roll on back". The "roll on back" takes some serious practice because timing is critical. When Wilbur suddenly bolts forward from that lizard, you'll roll on back off the saddle. You'll get up close and personal with the underside of his tail. Timing is critical because you don't want to experience one of Wilbur's three kicks while you are landing.

All saddles have a pommel. It's the front of the saddle that stops you in place when he stops fast enough to send you flying over his head. It's the part of the "U" that either keeps your privates safe or changes the tone of your voice. The deeper the pommel, the less likely you are to go flying over Wilbur's head when you try to airplane stop him with the shank bit, but you'll be more likely to need emergency ice, a diaper and some of that stuff that Wilbur uses to stay mellow. Western saddles have horns on the Pommels. Depending on how you ride, this can be very helpful. You can hang almost anything from them. Just put a loop on a bag of goodies and hang it over the horn. I have a tip, don't hang a large plastic trash bag used for beer cans. This could force you to test your auto-inflate breast protector when you go flying off his back. I learned this the hard way and found out how fast my horse, "Lightening Rod", could run. Also, I don't suggest you tie any kind of rope from the horn to yourself. Remember the discussion above about looping the rope around your hand or waist? Well, take that and add about 7 feet of flight before you land and get dragged. It won't be a bird or a plane, it will just be you. It will also be your friends watching and betting on how long it will take you to hit the ground and stop bouncing once Wilbur has stopped.

All styles of saddles also have a cantle. The cantle is the back of the saddle which also gives you a choice of height. How low do you want to go? How secure do you want to be? If you want to maintain that "don't go nowhere, no matter what happens" feeling of the "U" saddle, the cantle will be the same depth as the pommel. If you are feeling brave and you love the feeling of summersaulting off your horse's back end with three spins, one super loop and a final land, go low. If you go low, I highly recommend you take gymnastics, so you can learn how to gracefully use the "he's gotta go so I gotta back roll" technique. Another consideration for this part of the saddle is your roll. Let me explain, the deeper the cantle, the more it pushes your pelvis forward. The shallower the cantle, the easier it is to sit on your pockets. Your experienced trainer of one year will help you develop so you can properly ride on your "pockets". If you choose to ride with a deeper cantle, you'll need to work extra hard to keep from rolling forward on the areas of your body that may incur injury if you're riding in a "getter tough" Western saddle. I used to ride with a high cantle. To ride on my pockets properly, my experienced trainer (a nice young lady of 17 years old who had been riding since she was 16.5) put a wooden wedge in front, under my cooch to help keep me rolled on my pockets. Not a good idea. My dreams of becoming a porn star had to be put on hold for 72 years.

The seat of the saddle is very important, especially if you've paid a lot of money for butt implants. You need to be comfortable, and comfortable means soft on that derriere. The type of saddle can determine how much "soft" there is. If you want to ride the range, across the hills, through the cattle, pulling steers and look super tough doing it; you're not allowed much "soft". You'll need to be tough. You'll need to show your derriere can handle the Wild West and be tough showing you can handle it. When you climb into the western saddle, it should be a firm landing. Unfortunately, if you land too firm, you'll have to suck it up and wince, so no-one knows you just busted your pelvic bone. You want to look rough and tumble? The western saddle is the way to go (in addition to practicing your low raspy voice and clinking of your spurs). On the other end of the spectrum is the endurance saddle. This saddle is made for one of two things: 1) People who seem to have combined one too many energy drinks with expresso coffee and ride for miles and miles and miles and miles and miles and miles; or 2) People who are so skinny they must hold on to a tree when a breeze picks up. There is no meat on those bones. They need "cushioning maximus" and this is the reason why it's great to be a little overweight. The endurance saddle not only comes with automatic cushion but many times you can choose how much soft you want. Some of these saddles even come with actual seat options so you can switch them out. In between the Western saddle and the Endurance saddle, you have a full range of additional saddle seat choices based on how you will ultimately decide to ride. I say "ultimately" lightly because you'll change your mind about 1,000 times so you might as well pick up that midnight job now, so you can afford every saddle ever made and relive your initial multi-saddle investment.

In between the pommel, cantle and seat, you have a bunch of other stuff that makes up the rest of the saddle style. The design, shape, angles, length of things are all dependent upon your first style of riding interest. There will be multiple other choices for your saddle like how many D-rings do you want? If you plan to ride long hours out on the trails, you'll want 15 of these attached to each side, front and back, so you can put everything from your bathroom into little saddle bags and carry it with you on the trail AND still have room to tie on the beverage holders for your margaritas. How many strings do you want? These can be tied on to your D-rings so not only can you tie things directly on the rings but now you tie things with things you can tie. You'll have fender options (the things that go under your thighs and connect to your stirrups, you hope). You'll have stirrup options, the things you put your feet in that keep you in the saddle; or the things you put your feet through to make sure it's pretty when your foot gets stuck and Wilbur gets angry because he remembers you broke your promise and never gave him his organic apple. I could go on and on about all the choices you have between these described parts of the saddle.

Without encouraging you one way or the other, that's your trainer's job, there are some basic concepts and requirements to remember when looking at the different saddle choices:

- The Western: Must have a low raspy voice to match the spurs. You'll need to pad up in the front because you'll feel it if Wilbur decides to do an unplanned sliding stop when you're not ready. This saddle has a horn on it and the horn comes in various sizes. This is another example of "size matters". In this circumstance, the smaller the horn the worse it's going to hurt when you and your reproductive body parts slam into it. The good thing about the horn is that it will stop you before you flip over Wilbur's head. The Western saddle is also heavy. It's heavier when you have to pull it off and on while trying to adjust your saddle pad. This saddle has a lot of leather. It will be important to watch that leather. If it becomes brittle, it won't break until that critical moment when everyone is watching you canter Wilbur around the arena or out on the trail.

- The English or Dressage saddle: You can kiss the "U" goodbye. If you must ride in a "U" deep seat for this saddle, it will eliminate the ability for others to see you when you perfectly push up, sit down, push up, sit down, push up sit down (aka the post). This saddle needs a much smaller saddle pad and it has the added benefit of allowing you to fly further should you experience an unplanned dismount. It is important to remember to ride correctly when using this saddle. Timing is critical. You'll never want to be in "push" position when Wilbur sees that white bag across the arena. This saddle is much lighter should you need your grandmother to help you saddle up.

- The Treeless saddle: This is the ultimate stuntman saddle. It laughs at you and makes you believe you are truly secure. Now, what is missing on this saddle again, I lost my train of thought. OH!!!!! That's right, the tree. The tree is that reinforced bar that sits over the horses back. It may look like there is a tree but it's just the rest of the saddle with a note on the underside that says, "I forgot to include tree here." The treeless saddle does have a huge advantage, it will mold and shape to your horses back. It will mold to the side of your horse when you've slid to the left or right. It's especially effective for holding in place when you try to get on. With the treeless saddle, sometimes that pressure thing gets in the way. You pull, and it's goes with you, which gives you a reminder of the term "heading south".

If you are going to ride in a saddle, it's important to remember that thing that holds the saddle on, the cinch. Your trainer is going to tell you otherwise, because they want you to be balanced and that means no cinch, just the saddle. In my opinion, the cinch really adds to the options you have when you ride, like staying on. It's almost the finale to completing your saddle set up and is of upmost importance if you really want to keep the saddle on your horses back.

The cinch is another one of those confusing pieces of equipment that has 2,039 choices. The basic cinch is designed around the type of saddle you'll be using. You have your Western cinch, English cinch, and Dressage cinch. The basic difference between cinches is the connecting parts at the end. The western cinch has a metal loop with one prong to hold the saddle in place. The English, Dressage or Endurance saddle cinch usually has two separate buckles to hold the saddle in place. Again, several choices to follow but the biggest choice is size. This is another opportunity to reinforce that size does matter and material follows second.

Your cinch is your security. When you choose your cinch, make sure it's not a hoarder and likes to collect things if you go on the trail. Make sure it's 5 sizes too small when you put it on because it won't be when Wilbur gets warmed up and make sure, above all else, it matches the rest of your set up. There is nothing worse than seeing a cinch that's color doesn't match the saddle, geezers! Make sure you have extra cinches. Cinches can come apart at the most inconvenient times, like when you're riding in front of a bunch of people, trying to make an impression or when you are just ready to make a 4-point turn in the arena. Cinches are the magic to help decide your riding style preferences whether it's above the horse, on the side of the horse or underneath the horse.

No matter what the material choice, size matters for cinches. I learned early in life about how smart horses can be when I went off into the horizon with my trusted steed, "Tone Loco", we'll call him TL. TL was always perfect when I led him and saddled him. I followed a certain pattern which worked well for me: Lead horse out of stall, feed 1lb of carrots (they didn't have organic that long ago) as negotiation process to make sure he'd be good for the ride, put on saddle pad, take off saddle pad, put on saddle pad again, put on saddle and put on bridle. It was a simple process that seemed flawless and helped me get ready for a great ride. I would get out of sight of all other people and find a nice place to climb on. After a few failed mounting attempts, which usually resulted in my utter lack of height and ability to put my foot above my chest to reach the stirrup, I learned to climb on smoothly. TL was the perfect gentleman as he walked off. Back in those days, I wasn't very balanced. After about 20 minutes of riding I would feel myself start to lean to the left. I hadn't had my margarita yet, so I knew it wasn't me. TL would feel this leaning and start to move just a little faster and faster, but I'd still hold on. Just when I thought I could pull myself back up, I'd hear TL laugh a little and see him wink at the other horses. This was his cue to take 5 sudden steps to the right and I would slide down the left. I was smart though, I rode in a "U" saddle so I would still be hanging on even though I was on the side of TL instead of the top. Fortunately, I had my strings and D rings on the saddle, so this helped me stay on until the saddle dropped completely underneath TL. It was a good thing I snuck in some of that special "calming hay" before we rode. Otherwise, I would have watched TL run off into the sunset after I fell, only to see him slowly trample my custom made "U" saddle as the cinch broke.

How is this relevant to the size of the cinch? The cinch is magic, and the cinch can alter its state depending on its mood. The cinch has its own personality and it plans evil strategies with Wilbur at your expense. The trick about the size of the cinch is that it doesn't stay the same size after you put it on. It may start out at the perfect size, allowing your saddle to sit comfortably and tight enough so you won't wind up under his belly. But the minute you get comfortable after a bit of riding, the joke will start and the cinch will loosen. It will loosen just enough so you don't really know it's happening, but it won't be tight anymore. You won't know the size just changed because you'll be so busy feeling "as one" with Wilbur until Wilbur gets the cue from the cinch and he takes a turn to the right. You'll only see the cinch laughing at you when you wind up on Wilbur's side, just before you fall off. Therefore, size matters, cinches stretch and grow with excitement, so you need to be ready for the excitement. It's the size of the cinch, after Wilbur has walked around for a while, that will keep the joke from being on you.

Before you decide on the size of the cinch, you must decide what material to use for the cinch. Most of the cinches, regardless of style, come in a variety of material choices. You can get them in leather, mohair, fleece, wool, and neoprene. They each have their own pros and cons. The important thing is how comfortable they are for Wilbur and how much will they stretch. You'll also need to consider where you will be riding because material decides how much of the wild and thorny brush you bring back with you.

The Mohair cinch is a very popular cinch. It's got rope style strands which connect from the center to the connectors. Mohair can be any type of hair from wool to camel to synthetic. These days they are usually wool or synthetic. The rope style strands allow the cinch to breathe, which is supposed to keep your horse from getting too hot. The great thing about Mohair is that it doesn't bring back nearly as much debris if you accidently wind up off-roading with Wilbur when he decides to run you down a hill only used for deer. The bad thing is, this cinch has an exceptional sarcastic side and by the time Wilbur does decide to run you down that hill, it's already stretched out enough to ensure you'll be sideways hitting the bushes. If you stay on, you'll come back with more debris in your teeth than in the beautiful Mohair cinch.

Fleece (wool, cotton or synthetic) is another great possibility for a cinch. It's the little cloud of fluffy on Wilbur's underbelly. The fleece cinch doesn't have as much of a sense of humor, so it won't stretch as much. It's comfy and cushy, like the fleece saddle pad. If you use fleece, you don't need to take as much equipment on the trail because the fleece cinch is designed to help you collect things. It grabs whatever you may pass and keeps it securely in its grasp, embedding it as you ride, until you get back and are ready to unsaddle. Sometimes the fleece cinch feels exceptionally giving and finds the sharpest thorns and debris to store as close to your horse's stomach as possible, thus allowing just enough time for Wilbur to realize that the ends of the thorns coming from that fleece aren't going away so he'll make sure you do. Once a good thorn gets stuck in that fleece, the deepest saddle in the world isn't going to keep you there. If this happens and you've planned properly, you will have tied yourself on with the strings from the D-Rings and worn your tennis shoes, so you can stay connected and run with Wilbur as he bucks you off and bolts for home. He won't stop after you've been politely dismounted because Mr. Fleece cinch will just keep poking Wilbur all the way home.

There is also the Neoprene cinch. If the saddle is still moving with the neoprene saddle pad, heck, get the cinch too. No slide from the top and no slide from the bottom. Nothing says comfort like backward rub on the back with an added side of hair pulling from the bottom. Wilbur, now the angry horse, is giving you the finger for making him look like a surfer and has had enough of all this "cushioned" material that gets soaking wet and pulls his hair around in directions it should never go. Just like the saddle pad, the cinch will double ensure the saddle doesn't move so neither will you until Wilbur can take a sharp enough turn at the same time he kicks his back feet higher than a pine tree.

There are other equipment options that can be used on Wilbur, this is ancillary equipment that is necessary based on your possible riding interests. It's based on how you want to look when out in public. The breast collar can be used for keeping you from sliding off Wilbur's rear end when he jumps out of the arena or up that hill. It can also be highly decorative, so you can just wear it around with your matching Headstall that screams, "I'm da bomb." (Warning use breast collar when going up steep hills. Even better, set up a mattress at the bottom of the hill so you have something to land on when you roll off.) There are a variety of choices for gear that helps hold the horses head down. This gear is intended to keep the horse from throwing his head so high it ruins your recent nose job, rearing so high it ruins your recent buttock implants, collecting (that's why you put the carrot in the breast collar), or bolting (because everyone knows a horse with his head tied down can't bolt). There is the crupper. Horses love cruppers. Wouldn't you love something clinging underneath your wahoo and getting tight whenever you go downhill? Note: If you ride with a neoprene saddle pad and cinch, you won't need anything because nothing is moving anyway.

Of these gear choices we need to add in the "this helps it fit factor." If something doesn't fit, there are options to make it fit. After all, why buy something else when you can buy something more expensive that will help what you already have fit better? Saddle pads have lifts and dips. Lift to get it off the shoulders and dips to fill in the gaps. If the saddle is tight on the horse, there are extra lifted pads because a tight saddle needs more cushion to make it tighter. There are also special cinches made just for pulling the saddle up or down in any specific spot of the saddle. If the saddle really doesn't fit, it can be remedied by buying a lifted, extra thick pad (this will also help you look taller), with cut back shoulders (to help make sure Wilbur can run full speed when he gets tired of all of it) and a special "forward pressure" cinch to pull the back of the saddle down tighter and lift the front. Basically, you've just made yourself a rocket. Where you land there will be no Margarita's, but your horse will still look great and he'll be laughing from earth.

If this all gets too complicated, you run out of money, your saddle fit experiment injuries temporarily prevent you from being able to lift anything over 1.27lbs or you just want to bond with Wilbur and be as close as possible; you can opt to ride bareback, with a bareback pad or with just a blanket. Between the three choices, it's the same concept with only a few variables. The bareback pad has a cinch to hold the pad on, so it won't slip as easily when you start to slide. It also has something to grab on to should you start heading south. This little handle at the front of these pads works exceptionally well for gripping. Bareback pads are loyal to the end. They will gladly go with you when you slide down his side before falling off. Another benefit of the bareback pad is that will stay on if you get dumped so you won't have to go hunt for it when Wilbur has gone running off. If you insist on riding completely bareback, the best way to have a safe ride is to get Wilbur sweaty before climbing on. This ensures you don't slide as much when he starts doing one thing and your rhythm hasn't caught up yet. It's a nice feeling too. In my opinion, you're not a true horse person until you've felt the sensation of tiny, sweaty horse hairs poking through your jeans into your thighs. There's just no feeling like it and it's even better if you are crazy enough to ride in shorts. If you want to protect yourself from those hairs but you feel you're above needing any security just throw a blanket on. We'll rename Wilbur to "Chief Buck A lot". A simple blanket over his back adds more to the riding experience than any other type of riding. With a blanket, not only are you missing the security of having any grip or set up that will help stay in place, but you've put on something that would prefer to fly away. This type of riding will take at least 4 margaritas and two stacks of calming hay, so you won't feel yourself going for a magic carpet ride when the lizard spooks Wilbur and your blanket takes you on its own spectacular journey. Saddle blanket riders are brave and you should be too. If you can successfully ride like this, you'll be required to carry a flask with you and Wilbur's initials in an engraved heart. It will be braided into his mane for easy access and the callouses on your rear end will help make sure you stay atop no matter what kind of kite Wilbur turns into. YOU will be the one who can run from behind Wilbur and jump on. If you've had too many margaritas you may miss him entirely or jump over him, but nevertheless, you'll clear. And horses that can be ridden this way always have a sense of humor. They sense you coming and humor all onlookers by stepping to the side or forward when you're ready to practice your flying mount up.

CHAPTER VI-GET THAT GROUNDWORK GOING

Before you start riding, you should consider spending some time with Wilbur, training from the ground. Although your trainer has happily agreed to start training in your first of three saddles, you'd like to get to know Wilbur and see how he moves. Working with Wilbur from the ground will help ensure he'll know what you want by thinking it, just send him the message and he'll know. If you're on the ground, he'll see your eyes and those will tell him exactly what you want from him, so he can do the opposite. Plus, all the $75.00 training books say ground work is important, so it must be. There is no better way to bond then to spend time together on the ground. "Natural Horsemanship" is, without a doubt, the best way to train a horse. That means you naturally move together as if you were both the same, like watching the Nutcracker ballet with the added value of being stepped on. They learn to trust you, you learn to trust them. There are so many ways to do ground work with Wilbur. You can lunge him, teach him to direct and drive, teach him to circle around you, hand walk him everywhere and set up scary obstacles to lead him through. The ground work options are endless. And once you've gotten the groundwork, this transfers to the saddle and off you two go, into the horizon like a happily married couple.

The Lunge and Tangle

We discussed lunging earlier and the variety of ways you can practice dirt skiing. What is lunging? Lunging a horse simply means you attach a really long line to him and walk, trot and run him in circles around you. This is a great exercise for learning verbal communication and the art of you being directionally challenged. The goal is to hold your hand out while holding the lunge line in the direction you want to go and using a whip behind Wilbur to get him to move different speeds. Usually, the whip winds up in the wrong hand and the lunge line is tangled from the whip down to your ankles. Remember, the longer the line, the more to get tangled up with. Since Wilbur (or any horse) loves to run the same circle over and over and over, he'll do this for you for about 10 minutes. Once Wilbur is done, he'll do a few different things to let you know he's done. The first sign he is done is the direct eye contact. Yes, you two have been secretly communicating through the eyes but this is different; he'll tip his head into you and glare at you with the inside eye. You'll know this is not the same as the other look because you'll see just a hint of red glimmer in the center. By the time you realize something has changed, you'll notice his ears have already started to pin back against his head. You'll know both ears are evenly pinned because he's coming straight at you, still at the trot. This is Wilbur telling you that it's your turn to lunge, and you will, because he's bigger and knows you're tangled up in the line. The second way Wilbur may let you know he's done is simply leaving. Whether you're in a small arena or out in the open, he can still leave. If you're in an arena, he'll just go into a gait you can't possibly keep up with and he'll go faster and faster. If you are conditioned, you'll be able to just let the lunge line work around you without getting tangled up or having to spin. If you're lucky, you'll have to spin around in the center, trying to keep up with him so you don't get tangled. Don't be fooled by Wilbur, he knows what he's doing. When you get so dizzy you just can't hold on anymore and fall on the ground, he'll be there to stand over you and laugh at you, along with your friends. The "Drag and Tow" is another great lunge opportunity that takes a lot of practice, band aides, and margaritas. When first starting to lunge a horse, you drag him to where you want to go and he'll tow you to where he wants to be. While lunging him, you drag your feet as he runs crazy around you and he tows you down the rest of the rail when he's had enough of your dragging. The key to successfully lunging your horse is anchoring. You'll want to anchor yourself by digging your heels in and leaning back anytime you lunge Wilbur. This way you'll be ready for the perfect dirt skiing experience when he does decide he's done. It will look like you're skiing on purpose. Now, if he decides to run in toward you this technique may not work so well. Once you've mastered lunging in an arena, you'll want to take it outside the arena where there are no fences to stop either one of you. You may want to have your running shoes on. Lunging is a great way to learn how he moves, how many times he's willing to go around in circles and whether he'll move off pressure by running toward you or into pressure by pulling you everywhere when he's done.

Driving Mr. Wilbur

Have you ever seen, "Direct and Drive?" Since we all use our fingers to point in the direction we want our horses to go, direct and drive does just that. When you point your finger and slightly stoop over, Wilbur should go in that direction. It's important to note that the slight stoop of your body MUST be in synch with the finger point. Sounds like a simple process and since Wilbur has already connected with you on a telepathic level, you technically shouldn't even need to do this. Just to make sure your trainer is thoroughly impressed, you'll want to make sure Wilbur can "Direct and Drive." The steps are to hold the lead in the direction you want to go, pointing in that direction with the lead finger (remember the stoop). He should turn and go in that direction. If he doesn't, you'll add a little swing of the line on his back end and encourage him. Once you've got it, you can do all kinds of amazing tricks: you can

84

walk forward while he D&D's back and forth in front of you. You can D&D him through obstacles, you can D&D him around other horses, you can also get him to D&D around other people, and if you're successful, you'll get them tangled up instead of you.

Beginning the D&D needs coordination, buying more protective toilet paper and using the suggested breast protector. When you first start, Wilbur will be a little confused, so you'll need to use more encouragement from behind. A little swing of the end of the lead line towards Wilbur's rear end is sometimes required to help Wilbur understand your finger point. When you first start this, Wilbur may not be so keen on the hind end concept. You'll be just close enough to Wilbur for him to make contact when he decides to bequeath you the "angry" kick because he thinks you're being ridiculous. (You'll want the breast protector.) Sometimes he even adds insult by trotting off after you've been given the beautiful gift of the angry kick. Now, if you properly have the lead line wrapped around your hand, you know the hand your pointing the finger with, you won't have to worry about Wilbur trotting off because you'll still be connected. The D&D is a great way to show off and show everyone who doubted you, how amazing Wilbur is. He knows what you want just by the way you stoop, I mean point the finger. Once you get great at point that finger, you'll just need to stoop, look in the direction you want Wilbur to go and think it; Wilbur will know exactly what you want and do it.

Do You Want to Disco?

Disco 101 is my favorite form of groundwork. What? Never heard of it? Well, that's okay because I invented it. Disco 101 is, essentially, working to help Wilbur learn how to deal with the unexpected. This is so important because the unexpected things only happen when you are just climbing into the saddle or you are ready to start riding. Once you've mastered the Lunging and D&D exercises, you can't skip Disco 101. I used to do this with a lot of horses I trained.

Imagine that you're walking with Wilbur down the road and suddenly you break out dancing, jumping back and forth, waving your arms and singing "Staying Alive". If Wilbur is your BFF, he'll stay right next to you despite the desire to run in embarrassment. He'll be shocked and may try to lower himself to avoid being seen with you, but he'll stay. If Wilbur was named "Tone Loco" in a past life, he'll be running back to his old home the minute you raise that right arm to "Eh Eh Eh Eh Staying ...". Once he gets past the sudden, unexpected, random movements out of nowhere, you'll move on to other unexpected things. There are so many songs for this form of groundwork. You can use "I Just Can't Fight this Fleeing Feeling Anymore" for challenging obstacles, like flapping an umbrella over his head out of nowhere. Or, you can use, "The Beasts Come Out of Night" for when you walk him around a corner and lead him toward a hanging black rain coat that is swinging everywhere above his head. Disco 101 training is limitless. I used to create an obstacle course that consisted of a swinging umbrella tied to a tree, a hanging raincoat my horse would have to go under, a bunch of milk jugs tied together that would magically start dragging behind us after we passed them, and more. Disco 101 should not be part of training until you've mastered the art of holding on to the lead without wrapping your hand in it and confirming that Wilbur does understand you when you say "Whoa" because this will put the stop request into challenge. If you happen to get tangled up while practicing Disco 101, Wilbur will use you to make sure everything set out is brought back, because he'll drag you through them.

Time to Ride!!!!!!!!

CHAPTER VII-HOPPITY HOP INTO THE SADDLE

The most magical time for you and Wilbur is when you're ready to climb into the saddle and start that riding time. You've got the perfect gear for yourself, you've done all your groundwork, Wilbur can read your mind with a slight point of a finger, you've brushed him 22 times and you've got the perfect equipment. His bridle matches his reins that match his saddle that matches his cinch that matches the sparkling bling on the polish on his feet. It's time to ride! Riding is based on riding styles and that makes for a whole separate book, so we are really going to stick to the basics. It's a simple process: 1) Pre-Flight (I only mean that part literally) equipment check; 2) Get on (mount up); 3) grab your reins; and 4) use your feet to help guide him.

Pre-Flight, Hopefully Not, Check

The pre-flight equipment check is like making sure your zipper is up before you step out of the house. Don't open the door until you know all is secure. Check your and Wilbur's equipment. You can figure out your best order, but you'll need to make sure it's all in order, otherwise, you'll take direct flight.

First, check your saddle equipment. Have you set and reset the saddle 9 times to make sure the pad is still there? Have you looked behind Wilbur to make sure the pad isn't sitting on the ground? Are your stirrups still attached? Is the cinch tight? Has Wilbur been walked around for 2 hours so you could check and re-tighten the cinch?

Second, make sure the bridle is on, not the halter unless you've already proven the bond that says, "Wilbur will do anything for me with nothing on his head." Make sure the bit isn't backwards or upside down. You can easily test this by turning your head upside down and looking from that perspective. If you're looking from upside down and it looks like it's on correctly, it's probably wrong. Besides making sure the reins are correctly attached, you'll also want to make sure they aren't crossed when they go over Wilbur's head. If they are, it will take you a while to figure out why he keeps turning to the left every time you pull the right rein. That is, unless his name used to be "Kanya West".

The final important step is to make sure Wilbur is untied from the rail before trying to walk him off. If he suddenly stops and resists leaving the rail, it will either be because you forgot to bribe him before the ride, or he's still attached.

Friends, Feet and the Ground-What to Climb Up With

Before you ride, you must climb up! How you climb will be decided by your height, Wilbur's height and how often you go to Yoga classes. With these factors in mind, there are still so many choices you have to climb on and you can use different styles each time to figure out what works best for you. If you are 6 feet tall and Wilbur is only 14hh tall, you've got it made, just lift your foot over and move along. If you are 5'2" and Wilbur is 18hh, you may need to resort to other mounting techniques. In my vast experience of riding, I've learned that most of us are height challenged when we ride horses. Those stirrups seem to be just high enough to make it difficult to climb up. If not in the beginning, it will become difficult after you've gotten off and on a few times in a day.

The most common way to mount a horse is from the ground, you just put a foot in the stirrup and swing yourself over. This can also be challenging for taller people because they may swing right over. If you want to look as graceful as a ballerina every time you get on, there are some things that can make this look smoother. If you are height challenged, tall horse challenged, tired challenged or just older challenged; mounting from the ground becomes a little more "challenged". These challenges make it even more important to prepare for mounting from the ground.

Let's start with stretching. This is a great way to help improve mounting from the ground. It not only helps to increase your flexibility in lifting your leg to your chest or higher, but it also makes it easier to adjust when you need to ride a wide horse. For mounting purposes, upper leg stretching is the most beneficial. If you are already flexible, you can start at a more advanced level, but if you are just starting, you can use these steps to improve your flexibility.

Let's review some of the steps to improving your flexibility:

1. When you are doing anything that needs a few steps up, skip a few of those steps at the office or at home to increase the height of the step. (Use the leg you'll have to lift when mounting). Eventually work your way up to climbing a flight of stairs in three steps. Word of warning, keep a pillow or two at the bottom so you're protected when you miss that step.

2. Lift those legs. Stand when you are at work or working on computer projects. Start with resting your leg on your desk. If you are cooking or working at a counter, keep that leg on the counter. (Note of importance, if you are keeping your leg on the counter while you cook, make sure no guests see you and make sure there is no visible

dirt). Build up to lifting your leg and holding it next to your shoulder while you work on a project. A few added words of warning; make sure you are wearing stretch pants so there are no embarrassing rips and have something close to grab on to so, when you do fall (like a tree), you can catch yourself. It's better to do this in privacy. Just visualize the image if someone were to walk in while your leg is above your chest.

Strength training is also important for ground mounting. This process is much simpler. Simply use your mounting leg to lift yourself up and practice the "sit squat" exercise. Go in chair position when brushing your teeth, in the shower, while at a desk or any place you can think of. Again, it's important to have something to grab when you tip over, and you will. Also, remember there is no chair. I think that one is self-explanatory.

Mounting from the ground does come with some dangers. First and foremost, there is the obvious twist of the ol 'saddle. Remember when we discussed tightening the cinch? I am pretty sure most of us have experienced the horse version of the dance; put your leg into the stirrup and lift. You lift and saddle heads south. The good thing about this is that the stirrup is much closer to the ground. If you can get your leg in and push yourself and the saddle back into proper position, you should be famous. I guess this is the reason they always recommend tightening your cinch. If your saddle does slip while you are trying to mount from the ground, it is vitally important you make the "whoosh" sound as you crash to the ground.

The second danger is what I affectionately call the, "Foot stuck fall back." You've got your foot in the stirrup and suddenly realize you can't pull yourself up as you fall backward, landing on the ground, foot still in stirrup. This is a true test of your athleticism. Either you lay on the ground and pretend you're doing leg lifts while you subtly try to get your foot out of the stirrup from the horse that is looking at you like you're an idiot. Or, your horse is so very embarrassed, he takes off at a bolt. This is when you find out how fast you can run on your arms.

There is a final word of warning when mounting from the ground; those leg lift and flex exercises may make you stronger than you think. When pushing off to lift yourself up, don't over lift. This may cause you to completely miss the saddle and go crashing to the other side of the horse (thus, the reason experts recommend helmets), again leaving the horse to look at you in utter embarrassment while you lay on the ground trying to make this look like an amazing stunt.

The second choice to mounting is using a friend to help you get up. We'll call this the, "Love'em or Hate'Em" mounted aid program. "A friend in need, is a friend indeed." A very famous quote, no doubt. What if you are the friend in need and your need is a leg up onto your 4-legged friend?

This still applies to the height challenged, tall horse challenged, older challenged or just tired challenged people who've been riding the trails from a month to years. We've all experienced horse mounting challenges.

When preparing yourself for assisted mounting, there is only one exercise you need to do. It's called, "balance exercises". Perhaps this is good time to start Yoga. This will help with any kind of mounting technique you use. Get yourself used to balancing on one leg with the other leg lifted and bent in front of you (do you remember the "Karate Kid?"). While the other leg is lifted, jump on the one leg. You are ready for assisted mounted when you can do this without falling like a dead tree. Note of caution, don't practice this in the grocery store.

Now, let's look at the different techniques of "friend assisted mounting":

1) The straight up lift. This doesn't happen very often, so it only needs a quick description. This is when your very strong &/or tall friend decides the best way to get you in the saddle is by lifting you by your waist, straight up so you are high enough to swing your leg over. Do I need to discuss the hazards, besides your head landing in a branch, of this style of aid?

2) Single leg lift. We all have done this. Your friend cups his/her hands at a reasonable height and you put your off foot into it. While you lift your "swing over" leg, they lift their hands to help push you up. This can be done quite successfully when the help comes from someone else who knows how high they can lift.

   There is a primary hazard with this technique. I like to call it the "Fly over". A friend lifts too high, too fast. As you head up and begin to swing your leg over the saddle, you find yourself in continued upward momentum. Usually, by the time you realize this is happening, you're going too fast to tell your friend to stop or to grab something that will stop you. Up you go and over you go, right to the other side of the horse. Usually, you land head down (again, justifying the helmet). The good side is that your horse is still standing there because you never even made contact. The bad side is that your friend has walked away like they were never involved, or they are laughing so hard they are buckling over, either way they aren't any help to you and you need to find a new friend with a slower lift speed.

   There is also a secondary hazard, although not as common. I affectionately call this the "Cheerleader". You know when cheerleaders jump in the air, creating a "Y" frame with their legs as they raise their arms? Consider this the cheerleader above the saddle. Imagine this; they lift, but by the time you realize they are going up too high and too fast, you've already assumed "over the saddle position". Usually it's the same outcome, landing on the other side, head down, horse who is still there and friend trying to escape.

There is one final consideration, it's the friend who thinks they are stronger than they are. When they lift, and you fully expect to get enough height to swing your leg over, but the lift just isn't quite high enough. By the time you realize you are getting nowhere near the top of the saddle, you are slamming into the side of it. The mounting leg is somewhere off to the north, your face is sliding down the side of the saddle to the south and your friend is headed east or on the ground because you've landed on them.

3) The knee push. Your friend gets down on one knee, you use that knee as a step stool. Push off with the closest leg to swing your leg over.

The first hazard (maybe it's not the first but it is to me because I've done this about 2,573 times) is the "under estimation crash". In your mind, you think you are pushing yourself high enough to swing over but, you crash into the saddle like a bird flying into a window. Although your scrambling and grabbing for something to help you, it's too late and you're already headed south. Sometimes, you may be lucky enough to land on your helpful assistant, who was not only there to help you up, but turned out to be a great cushion.

The second hazard isn't as common. Let's call it the Lift/Take down. Simple description; you step up, you push off, and as you push off your lift leg slips and you go tumbling down on your helpful assistant. I think this may contribute to the divorce rate amongst equestrians. Usually both of you land underneath your horse, who steps to the side and walks off in embarrassment.

4) I saved the best for last, the "butt lift". This isn't something you visit the plastic surgeon for, and it usually costs a lot less (some may offer to pay you). Sometimes, it's even enjoyable, depending on who's doing the lifting. Your willing "lifter" helps to lift you up and pushes your rear to help you get higher for clearance.

I am going to tell you a true story. I know it's true because it happened to me. First, I need to tell you that I usually ride in shorts. I love riding in running shorts. As a competitive rider, I get off a lot and hike, so I am in shorts and running shoes (don't worry, I have baskets, so I don't get my foot stuck). I have some great workout shorts that I wear under my running shorts. This is just to make sure everything stays where it should.

One day I went on a relaxing group ride with some friends. Since it was going to be an easy, short (I mean distance) ride, I rode in just my running shorts. I was on a very narrow trail when I dropped my camera. I jumped off to grab my camera and realized the trail wasn't wide enough, nor was there something for me to climb on, so I hiked down to the bottom of the hill. As the group waited for me to find a rock, a nice gentleman offered to give me a "leg up". He explained that he'd help push me up. I (very nicely) refused and thanked him for his offer, but my friends insisted I let him help. I was very apprehensive for two reasons: 1) I had nothing under my running shorts and 2) his plan was to help me via the "butt lift". I gave in and accepted his offer after about 5 minutes of my friends pushing.

Before letting him help me, I mentally planned what I needed to do. I needed to let him lift, keep my legs as close together as possible until the last moment and swing myself over in a forward manner so I could swing my leg after there was a risk of any exposure (literally).

It was time, errgggghhh... he got my foot in one hand, lifted and pushed my rear right up. The problem was that he lost his balance just a bit which pushed me back. I had to swing my leg early to avoid completely missing the horse. Well, there were multiple outcomes to this:

1) Friends realized the bathroom wasn't close enough because they were laughing so hard.
2) I had to apologize for the unplanned, rated R show.
3) I had a standing offer for the rest of the day for this type of assisted mounting.

I think I've made my point about this type of mounting assistance and probably why they say to make sure you have clean underwear.

These are the three most common types of human assisted horse mounting techniques. I'm sure there are more and if I think of them, I may even add another part to this series (lucky you). No matter what type of assisted mounting you choose, remember to use someone you know and trust. It's also important to make sure they are too committed to leave you if something happens or it's someone you don't care about that much.

Now, go find your future lifter and practice that flying technique.

Another possibility to mount is to use an inanimate object. Let's face it, many of us trail riders do experience the need for aid when out on the trails. The arena offers a much better choice of choosing your mounting help but, out on the trail, there may be only a few choices unless you've been able to tie your trainer and drag them with the custom D-ring you put on your saddle. Based on the other two options, it may be better to use an inanimate object to hoist yourself up. There are a wide variety of choices for mounted help inanimate object tools, like rolling logs, tree stumps, fences, bee hives, sides of hills that become loose dirt and tilt-y rocks that you don't know tilt until you've already got one foot in a stirrup. This style of mounting is an art and it takes practice on several levels. First, you must learn how to identify the potential of a true mounting object. Some will fake you out. Sides of hills are great because they look and feel solid and just when you get your foot into the stirrup and start to push yourself up, the hills will crumble, and you'll find yourself under Wilbur, looking up at his privates (realizing you forgot to brush there), with your one foot still in the stirrup. The best way to test the soil is to jump a lot before you put that foot in the stirrup. Wilbur will be okay because you did Disco 101 training with him. Stumps or logs can be another tricky one because they will look secure and they'll even hold in place while you try to push it around before stepping up on it. It won't move at all. The minute you put your foot in the stirrup and re-angle your other foot to swing up, you'll find out that it doesn't stay in place! If it's a log, it will roll. This will have a few different scenarios:

- It will roll toward Wilbur, you'll try to keep your foot on it, rolling with it like one of those log-jammer-men. It won't be until it's gone underneath Wilbur that you slide with it, your other foot coming back out of the stirrup resulting in you crashing underneath him. Don't worry about the log, it already rolled away. Remember, if you properly trained Wilbur, he'll just stand there. If you're in tennis shoes, your foot will still be in the saddle, but he'll still be standing there (because you've telepathically sent him a message to stand there).

- It will roll away from Wilbur! Oh, I hope you practiced your yoga. The more you've practiced, the wider your legs will be able to stretch between the one foot in the stirrup and one foot on the log. And yet, somehow, you'll manage to still hold on to the saddle so when you finally do fall on your face, you'll slide down the saddle, still gripping whatever you can. And, of course, Wilbur will be laughing his tail off.

Climbing up with the help of a stump is safer but still has its own hazards. Usually, it's a nice solid piece of wood, at least it looks like that. If the ground below is unstable, you won't know it until you're ready to put your foot in the stirrup. Apparently, lifting one foot makes you heavier so as you lift your foot up and start to lean, the stump starts to sink to one side. It will happen just quick enough, so you won't have time to put your foot down, but you will have time to get up close and personal with your beautiful new saddle. You'll see it close up as your face lands on the side of the seat and slides down, with a brief stop as your nose gets caught in the stirrup before you land on the ground. If you have any leg injuries, you can lay there for a while because your foot will still be elevated on the stump. The higher the stump, the faster you'll slide down the saddle.

Another stump hazard is when the whole inside of the stump is disintegrated because of termites. Since you are a safe rider and you hold the reins while you go to climb on, you'll at least be able to somewhat hold on because this happens quickly. You won't even have a chance to lift your foot up, the minute you start to lean to lift it will start to crumble beneath you. Usually this is an even crumble, so your face won't meet Wilbur's saddle. Since you'll just start to fall, you'll wind up holding Wilbur's front leg since you're still holding the reins and they are now pulling you forward.

When you are riding in the arena, you have a few other mounting options besides ground mounting and friend mounting. If you are brave enough to let your friends see you, you can always climb on Wilbur from the fence. Have your margarita sitting on a post because if Wilbur moves, you'll be face planting and your one leg will still be on the fence. The good thing is that you won't get your foot stuck in the saddle because it never reached that far. The other possibility is using that cute plastic step up. I am going to give you a tip; teach Wilbur to get used to the sound of that plastic step up, trust me. If you don't you, will not only find yourself on the ground, but you'll get a bit of the drag and tow because Wilbur will move away a bit faster than just a sidestep. He'll pretend he's scared. Again, have your margarita ready, that one will hurt.

CLOSING

Once you've mastered the steps of the pre-flight exam, the mounting process, and realized your trainer, who's been riding for a year, may not be the one you want; you're ready to really start riding. Sure, you've already dabbled with the riding. You've learned how to ride bareback, fly over Wilbur's head, do a summersault off Wilbur's rear end, and ride sideways. You've learned what happens when Wilbur doesn't want to stop, and you hold the reins at your shoulders. Now, you officially know what to do and what to wear (Reminder: breast protector, motorcycle mask and toilet paper wrapped around your body, steeled tipped shoes with heels). You and Wilbur can do anything together. You've brushed him 22 times, taken the saddle on and off 9 times, and made sure to lunge him the 10 minutes he'll tolerate it. Off you go into the sunset. You and Wilbur can do anything together and you can do things apart. Either way, you're officially a horse person and, if you were already experienced, you will just appreciate how much money you'll save in the future because these fun topics just reminded you of the crazy things you do. I know I do.

Have fun and be safe. And, remember to buy another one of these books for your friend who wants to buy a horse just like yours.

54221020R00066

Made in the USA
Middletown, DE
13 July 2019